# NINE AMBER PIECES

by

# Francis Voignier

Cover design by Francis Voignier
Artwork by Nadja/iStock © 2015

This book is a work of fiction whose characters should bear no resemblance with real individuals. The same goes with private places and businesses. All coincidences are hence deemed to be purely accidental.

Library of Congress Cataloging-in-Publication Data
Voignier, Francis 1954 – United States
Nine Amber Pieces/Francis Voignier
ISBN-13: 978-1-952858-00-0
ISBN-10: 1-952858-00-3

Fiction – Mystery – Crime – Intrigue – Action

francisvoignier.com
Dolosse & Writs, Eureka, CA

# CHAPTERS

# FROM THE AUTHOR

I never thought fiction writing in the first person was for me. I actually disliked the concept, finding it too egocentric to serve the reader in a balanced way. Then came Janet Trudy Smyth in *Story of a Tale-Maker* that changed it all for me—it opened doors I never imagined existed, in the process of which I felt liberated from the position of seeing my writing from above—I was now inside.

At the exception of two chapters, *Nine Amber Pieces* sets the tone for a repeat, as I again find myself inside the main character.

Whether I have found a new voice or not, I can't say, but I see why I would want to further explore the concept providing it keeps flowing in the right direction; of course, the right direction simply being the joy of the process. The travel is the destination.

Time is ultimately the test!

*Francis Voignier, 14th October, 2019*

My deepest thanks go to my life partner,
Reverend Elisabeth Zenker,
for her love and support, and to my dear friend,
Bruce Malamut,
for his guidance and inspiration.

# 1 – THREE BOXES

Klaus Nussbaum placed three small boxes on the coffee table.

"Each contains an identical set of three items that have been shuffled for safety. In other words, they'll need matching again. Take them; you'll know what to do with them when the time comes—good luck!"

He left without saying goodbye.

I didn't bother asking—I rarely did. Without checking their contents, I put the boxes back in their Pelican case, got up, and locked the apartment. I didn't expect to return to it any time soon.

It was just another assignment like all the others, but unlike any of them, save for my first one perhaps, I felt a tad apprehensive as if something had slightly shifted in the back of my mind—a near-imperceptible tremor that signaled some churning below the surface—hopefully, it was nothing beyond having been away from the big jobs for the last few years.

I drove out of Seattle towards Mt. Rainier, not really sure it was where I needed to go. Anyway, it felt like the right thing to do, plus I had nowhere to be in particular; not until I put my things in order and figured out the story about the items in the boxes. I hadn't been out of the city for a while; actually, I hadn't been out of my apartment much since my case partner, Jillian, was shot dead across the street from it.

Jillian's brother, Clark, owned a house in Greenwater along the Chinook Pass Highway. He seldom visited since his work tied him to L.A.; so with time, I was put in charge of keeping an eye on it. In truth, the neighbors were the rightful watchers. It was where I was going to spend the next few days, a place in between places. I always enjoyed my time there, but I never felt I could truly settle in such a small community—too many curious eyes.

Following a couple of drinks and the latest updates from the regulars at the local tavern, I headed for the house to fire up the service panel and turn on the propane. A shower and an early night were in order. There was much to get my head wrapped around concerning the assignment—a lazy evening was a rare luxury.

I was tempted to open the boxes, but I knew that if I did, I would end up spending the night wide awake. I settled for the *New Yorker* before shutting off the light.

— o —

I was up early and immediately went out for a stroll along the White River. I liked a clear head before breakfast and prior to beginning with the mind-bending process of deciphering what hadn't been said. It was obvious, by some of Nussbaum's well-manicured innuendos, that the new assignment would demand extraordinary focus; hence, I intended to start on the right foot. The right foot, in this case, meant a meticulous approach to mapping the larger picture. But not quite yet since the gurgling of water amid nature's awakening was the only focus I presently cared for.

The coffee shop was busy with characters heading for the mountains. The skiing season wasn't upon us yet; not with the heat of a long summer tailing off into an exceptionally balmy fall. No, most were hikers squeezing in a last chance at catching some colors and communing with the wild before the snow closed down the show. Well, there were also the two guys sitting in one corner, fitting neither local profile nor that of wilderness lovers. City folks, for sure, by the way they dressed, and without a viable reason to conduct business in these parts. It took me mere seconds to tag them as feds not giving a damn about their appearances, and in this case, seeming to relish sticking out like obvious outsiders. I absorbed the impunity as a message intended on revealing their origin, as the result of which they no doubt appreciated I noticed.

So, it had already started. I hadn't the foggiest idea about the assignment, yet the game was on. One of the men got up.

"Do you mind, Frank; it's Frank, right?" he asked, pointing to the empty chair.

"Be my guest; I gather I don't need to introduce myself."

"By the sound of it, you don't seem to care about who I am, or do you?"

"If you haven't said your name by now, I'm sure it's of no consequence. What makes you think I'm supposed to be interested in what you're about to tell me, or inclined to answer your questions?"

"It all depends on how much you care about your life. But I get it, Frank, you always work solo. Here's my number in case you change your stance!"

He handed me his card and walked back to rejoin his partner—he never used the chair. The two left in a white electric sedan in the direction of Rainier. I guessed my instincts had taken me to the right neighborhood. It seemed the case was intent on placing a few early pieces ahead of the real work—it was all good by me.

I glanced briefly at the card—just a name, Lazarus C. Mace, and a cell number with a D.C. area code. The feds alright, and with a name like Lazarus, no wonder he didn't seem to give a shit—that was the impression.

— o —

I finally spilled the content of one box on the kitchen table. Three two-inch-tall amber tetrahedrons— light to dark, each with an insect trapped inside—stood on one of their four triangular faces. Same with the other two boxes; the three sets looked identical. The only noticeable differences were the sizes and positions of the insects, but they all appeared to belong to the same species. I made sure to keep the groups apart from each other—safety was the keyword—no messing around.

Although artifacts trapped in amber were quite common, the pyramidal shape was new to me. But then again, I wasn't knowledgeable-enough about amber objects to come to a useful conclusion; that was Jillian's area. Damn, why did she have to die?! I so missed her, her ways, and her brilliance—of course, she would have had something to say about the figures on the table.

Nussbaum had simply said that I would know of their use in due time. The assignment presented itself as a riddle orbiting around them—an enigmatic core out of which I was to extract meaning in order to build a case. Later, I would figure out how to bring it to its conclusion. It was an inversion, practically a backwards assignment figuratively asking me to keep an eye on time's traffic across the median lane. For now there was only stillness, nine unmoving parts that knew of the storm ahead—they might even be the storm ahead! It was a simple matter of resetting their order at the right intersection. The gears were slowly meshing.

—— o ——

I swapped my city wheels for Clark's Jeep. Even without snow, the mountain roads were treacherous— nothing like puncturing a gas tank while driving over a rock to make you think twice about underrating the preciousness of commonsense.

I had no idea what I was going to find along backcountry roads, especially when I wasn't looking for anything specific, but I trusted something would pop up somewhere. I belonged to the school which believed that even in the absence of clues, clues were present—a relaxed, deductive way of evaluating the line of sight. The practice had come in handy on many assignments when the role of the observer far outperformed the ways of those caught on the inside tracks. Distance was key when one relied on surprise to succeed. That also explained why I was still alive in spite of Lazarus's foreboding remark. But there still was the unexplained tinge of apprehension that lingered. I told myself, then, to heed the winds that came from odd directions.

# 2 – BUSINESS DINNER

I packed food and water; left the house at eleven. At noon, after a quick lunch stop, I ran into the white Tesla parked in a pullout area ahead of the Crystal Mountain Boulevard intersection. It was the second lead in a row from the feds. I turned and shortly brought the four-wheeler to a stop behind a gravel pile—out of sight. It only took minutes before Mace and his sidekick flew by—I gathered they had seen me head this way. I began to wonder why they wanted me there, but how in the world did they know I was going to be driving Clark's Jeep? That was what I meant about small communities when I said "too many eyes"—someone was always ready to play informant, as in a make-believe game for adults. I felt sorry for those falling for the trickery of old dogs. Did the feds take them into, *ahem*, full confidentiality too? Of course, they did!

I booked a room at the Silver Lodge. It wasn't the plan, but as I insinuated earlier, I was at the mercy of an assignment in the making—when in need of enlightenment without light, extemporize!

I was relieved to find an open bar on the premises, even though I didn't drink. I ordered a virgin-something, seeking to engage in small talk with the bartender, mostly to probe him for unusual spikes in his routine. That was how I learned that a group of "important-looking" people had dined at the restaurant the last three nights. To me, it was simple: "important," in these parts, might as well have meant "dangerous," especially with the feds sniffing around. Since when did people of importance seek to meet in the middle of nowhere, unless there was something they needed to hide?

"Important as in royalty, show business, or plain business?" I asked

"Definitely straight business—serious stuff, no fun."

"Fun is for Vegas; what's in Crystal Mountain that purvey these business sorts a greater sense of seriousness—new lodges, high-tech gondolas?" I asked quasi-rhetorically.

"You're a cop, right? Don't tell me you're not!"

"Nah, merely a philosopher going through an existential crisis—right when I thought I had figured out the meaning of life."

The bartender was about to demonstrate his gift of repartee when the feds walked in to join us at the bar.

"I guess it's not too early for happy hour!" Lazarus blurted out, looking at my untouched cocktail.

"The more the clowns, the merrier! Your friend has a name or does he just sign with an X?"

"Sorry, Frank, he prefers to do the talking with his piece, but so that you two can cozy up later, he likes to be called Gomez, even though his first name is Dano."

"Nice one—Frank Marks—but you already know that!"

The bartender returned to his bottles, pretending they needed rearranging. He had gotten his chance at defining the difference between cops and philosophers. Even if he didn't believe me, he now had perspective he didn't have a moment before. That was what life was made of—snippets of unpredictability, even though I believed unpredictability was just a cover for choices with a sense of wicked humor.

Lazarus and Gomez settled for a couple of low grade brews, but before they had a chance to lay the first question, I hit them with one of my own.

"It seems we're in town for the same convention. Let me guess; you're in for the Gondolas, no?"

"Fuck you, Frank; you wouldn't know the first thing about lifts! You're here because we want you here, and you don't have the foggiest idea why!"

"Could be, but you wouldn't know why I would want to be here all the same; am I wrong?"

"What?!" Gomez ejaculated, confused.

"Let's just be assholes and have a pissing contest," I suggested.

"OK, Frank, you win; what do you have?"

"You want me here because you count on me finding what you're looking for, and when I'm done, you'll shut me down so that you can call it your own—typical of your kind, no? Must be important to the bureau to let the meter run on a couple of crackerjacks like you guys; so why don't we talk about the suits conducting business in this resort, when everyone else is having fun frolicking in the high meadows?"

By then, we had moved to a table away from earshot. The bartender was by far my biggest concern due to the extra abilities offered by his job. By that I meant a trained ear and the skill set necessary to recognize pertinent data and perform deductive evaluation of its content—in other words, the kind of stealthy nosiness that required training to detect. The way I saw it, "never give anything to anyone willing to ask or say too much!"

"Do you know anything about suits, Gomez; I sure don't?" Lazarus wisecracked.
"I'll ask my tailor when I see him!"

I realized we weren't going to get anywhere soon. These guys couldn't give me anything because they needed Frank Marks to show them the way. The only asset they had over me was the location—likely part of the instructions handed down from a higher operative level with a better view of the case. But now that we were there, the bureau's foot soldiers had no clue on how to proceed. I was the target until they moved onto a new one. In a nutshell, I just had been gifted the kind of official deadweight that would eventually expose me to the scrutiny of those I needed to hide from. Any way I shook it, I had to get these goons off my back.

— o —

All seemed perfectly in place when I arrived for dinner. The feds were sitting in a back corner, while in the middle of the room, six men and three women were gathered around joined tables piled with food and margaritas. Diagonally from Mace and Gomez, another two men in their thirties—undoubtedly bodyguards— were also keeping an eye. I had reserved a place close to the entrance which positioned me a short distance from the heavies. On the downside, the restaurant was busy and loud, effectively jamming the vibe emanating from center stage. I dressed casual, with the intention of blending with the regulars. Unwisely, the feds, either out of sheer bravado or plain stupidity, stuck to the side of arrogance, putting the bodyguards on alert. Maybe Mace had his reasons in opting to make the group aware they were being watched, but from my perspective, he was asking for trouble.

I observed the gathering in short spurts, never looking directly at anyone. I couldn't help notice there were three distinct subgroups involved: three ageless Asian women, one with a bleached Mohawk; three white males in their fifties; and three elder gentlemen, possibly from India. They all appeared exceptionally fit. Of course, I was in possession of three sets of amber figures which begged of me to heed the odd parallels. Besides a few exchanged smiles and a general demeanor that exuded an air of history within the group, the conversation generated no audible spikes. They appeared relaxed, something that couldn't be said of the bodyguards who scanned the room intensely in rhythm with arrivals and departures, as well as bathroom traffic. I caught them looking in my direction only once. I gathered the feds hadn't compromised me quite yet, but I couldn't let the notion distract me—too many had fallen to the double-sided blade of false positives.

My idea of arriving late for dinner as opposed to early, was more a matter of tensions than it was of a lack of timeliness. I preferred observing my subjects after they were properly settled in, rather than me being there when they reflexively scanned the space upon arrival—a simple matter of eliminating the palpable staticity of apprehension, a state that made them more suspicious of their environment. When the party finally left, I was in position to get a close look at each of them without so much as a modicum of weariness towards my presence—I had been absorbed as part of the decor. The head and tail guards barely gave me a blank look as they exited the room. The feds quickly followed.

——— o ———

# 3 – MS. OSHIRO

I opted to sit at the bar instead of aiming for my room. Something was telling me there was more to collect before calling it a night. The feds were nowhere in sight, which I took as them being busy doing their job. I still doubted they knew what they were looking for, but I came to think that perhaps they had more on the group than I had first imagined. My intuitions leaned towards caution, mostly because *the nine* hadn't given me the impression of delving in the usual business of crooks. There was an element of sophistication about them that betrayed an acute awareness of what they were conducting—these people didn't take chances. Yet, if Nussbaum and the feds were on them, it most assuredly meant something had transpired, but I had a hard time conceiving it was as the result of negligence, or a mundane accident—it practically smelled of purpose.

There were now two bartenders—my guy and a red hair with a sparkle in her eye.

"Hey, you're back! Something harder perhaps?"

"No thanks, I'll stick to the side of caution; whatever you served me this afternoon will do!"

"So, the two other dudes, philosophers as well?" he asked with a wink, sliding the drink towards me.

"Just guys I met this morning—not my crowd."

"I'll believe the philosopher bit if you admit those were undercover cops looking for trouble."

"Listen who's probing here!"

"You don't have to tell, but you may not want me to walk out of here with the wrong assumptions."

"I wouldn't. Let's just say you're as warm as you'll ever get—not my kind as I mentioned."

"Cool enough! So, what do you think of the group—business or pleasure?"

"Probably a bit of both. I tried not to stare; although I must admit I couldn't ignore the three Asian women—something rather classy about them."

"Is that all you came up with?! What about the men, do they look like the fun type to you?"

"You're probably right, but since we've got nothing better to do, please enlighten me on why you think they're here on heavy business."

"For one thing, I see lots of different people, business kinds and all, but mostly hikers, skiers, and honeymooners—I swear I've never seen a group quite like them before, as if they were a closed thinking unit."

"You actually mean a hive consciousness? Don't you think it's a bit out of the box?"

"Sure it is—that's the fun of it, man!"

This guy, Jeremy, was onto something, but I wasn't sure where he came from with it. Same as the feds, he seemed to be leading me closer to the assignment, challenging conventionality. But unlike the feds, who had nothing to say, he wanted me to see the group as he did: an odd cliquey bunch that didn't belong here.

I could have asked myself all kinds of questions, but I had lost my taste for speculations after my back got slammed to the wall on too many occasions. The cockiness of assumption was the bile under the sweet—

you could only taste the bitter so many times before the finish became you—either that or you were dead.

I was one of those who saw life as a series of opportunities better grasped before they were gone, hence why every one of Jeremy's words gained meaning and traction. We weren't dealing with regular business characters, or people. A hive consciousness in clusters of three sounded about right to me; except that such a thing wasn't suppose to exist.

"Jeremy, I'm curious; can you tell me what fascinates you about these guys; is it the novelty, the enigma—something offsetting the boredom in your life?"
"Is that the philosopher asking?"
"Who else?"
"It's not that they fascinate me as much as I enjoy talking with you. I miss conversations that don't need to lead anywhere, unlike those purported to go somewhere that never do. These people are my excuse to interact with someone funny and sober to boot."
"You just killed the suspense, but I'm with you—a toast to directionless conversations!"

— o —

I was expecting to bump into Mace and Gomez at breakfast, but they were nowhere in sight. Not that I cared much, but the thought crossed my mind about what they might have expected to find by following the group. Sure, there were details such as which of the three or four lodges they were staying at, the cars that drove them there, and what they did when they weren't having dinner at my hotel; all pertinent data that had their place amid the bureau's investigational methods, but which I found particularly irrelevant at that point. Where the group came from was what I needed in order to get to what they were about. Surely, the bartender had an idea about it.

I was daydreaming about Jillian when one of the three Asian women sat at the table in front of me. She didn't seem to be expecting company judging by her choice of seating, and as it so happened, we ended up facing each other. We briefly smiled when our eyes crossed, nothing but a flash, but I had no doubt it was all she needed to figure me out. It took me just as much to determine that the smile and eye clarity belonged to someone with razor-sharp focus, keen intelligence, and determination to spare. That woman was light years ahead of the pack, and I assumed the same applied to the rest of the gang. Just then, I wondered if she had sensed my quick evaluation of her persona.

As if to answer my question, she caught me scanning the space next to her, prompting me to look at her once more. It was clear we had connected at a level I was familiar with—the world of the intuitive. This time, her smile contained an invitation, as in having recognized a kindred spirit. I returned the greeting, refraining from deeper exploration. She left immediately after answering her phone. I only intercepted one word, a name: Vancouver—enough to understand where both our businesses would soon be taking us. She brushed by, close enough to leave an imprint of what her body would smell like in an intimate setting, a tinge of the wild teamed to an exotic fragrance I was unable to put a finger on, something savage, forbidden, intoxicating; a lead into an unknown I intuited would test me to my limits. For a second, I touched on a greater aspect of my own—whatever that meant.

— o —

It was pretty quiet at the bar when I swung by at around 2:00 p.m. Jeremy was at his post, dusting bottles and wiping surfaces.

"Virgin Mojito, Frank?"

"Please! By the way, what do you say we resume with our conspiracy theory about the mysterious nine—the hive people?"

"I say we play. As you may observe, I'm beyond bored!"

"I saw one of the pretty Asians all by her sweet self over breakfast. We didn't speak, but I practically got a taste of her from just being around."

"Powerful, man, that's why I can't help keeping an eye on them; I even retrieved some of their names from the registry!"

"You what?!"

"My friend Tilda, the red head, got them for me; she double shifts between here and their lodge."

"For what purpose?"

"You never know; Frank, someone might ask."

"For the heck of it, let's pretend I'm asking..."

"Depends on how well you can describe her."

"The sexiest of the three by barely a nose."

"Assuming we agree on the definition of sexy, she registered under Ms. Homura Oshiro, from Vancouver, British Columbia."

"And I presume you have all of their names memorized?"

"Not really, but I could get them for you later."

"Not that it matters, but I may want to socialize, should they decide to stick around a bit longer."

"They'll be here for the next couple of days, if that helps."

"It might—I may bump into Ms. Oshiro again; who knows?"

"Somehow I have the feeling you will," Jeremy said without elaborating.

I got what I wanted and more. Suddenly, I felt the need for fresh air. I left Jeremy to a boisterous group of hikers, promising to be back later for the list, even though I felt compelled to not honor my words. I was becoming conscious some greater force was in play and that more caution was required of me. The tug of the assignment was challenging my notion of natural balance—I had to regroup.

——— o ———

# 4 – CLOSER VIEW

I hadn't come across the feds since they went after the group the night before. I walked to the main lot where the white sedan was still parked. I guessed they had decided to hit the trails, but I doubted they had spent the night in the wilderness. Likely they had switched their accommodations over to the out-of-the-way bed and breakfast at Gold Hill where *the nine* had taken residence—a rather nervy move on their part. Again, we were dealing with a methodology short on subtlety. At any rate, I sensed trouble for the two.

I chose to have dinner at the inn across the lodge, aiming to put some distance between me and the various players. I couldn't ignore the links that tied *the nine*, the feds, and the bartender to each other—although I refrained from thinking I was being set up. I preferred to visualize the scenario as one whose pieces responded to the laws of attraction; thus, I accepted my position as being in the right place at the right time, as long as I stayed within the relative safety of the eddy.

But the rapids were oh so close, as I witnessed Ms. Oshiro entering, accompanied by one of the bodyguards. She instantly recognized me; flashing a broad smile as if to someone she had come to trust. I returned the friendliness, allowing the protective layers of the self to keep me steady. She sent her companion away, confidently walking towards my table. Aside from thinking events were happening faster than anticipated, I wasn't surprised. In the back of my mind I had imagined the encounter to be set for the next day, but I guessed the bartender's signal was received with much anticipation. It was obvious Jeremy had been one of the cogs all along; I sensed it the minute he suspected me to be a cop.

Homura Oshiro could have been in her early forties, or much older, or even substantially younger; it was hard to tell. Her age was more determined by her energy than it was by her looks—she was beautiful, but her inner radiance betrayed years beyond youthfulness.

"My name's Homura Oshiro; may I join you? I won't be offended if you prefer your privacy, Mr. ...?"

"It's Marks, Frank Marks; no, please, I could use the company."

"It's just that I'm somewhat lost away from the city, so I figured, why not engage with a new face? You look like someone I may like."

"Thank you, but why me; aren't there other likeable faces in this resort?"

"Yes, there are, but I already know them since we came together on business. Otherwise, it's no."

"Who would have thought? But then again, I haven't been looking around—I'm delighted you chose me though."

"I'm staying at the BnB on top of the hill— nothing there. I've gone on short hikes with my friend Hans who accompanied me here, but I'm afraid to say even that has lost its novelty. May I call you Frank?

"Please do. I gather it's OK to call you Homura, if I may?"

"Yes, of course, it stands for 'flame'—ouch!"

"I know not to play with fire, but it's a lovely name all the same."

"Thanks, Frank. Enjoying the pristine mountain air, or do you have other matters bringing you here?"

"Interesting you should ask, but sincerely, I believe that I'm here more on a whim than by choice."

"Nobody ends up where they don't choose to be; don't you know that?—I think you do."

"Nothing I can hide from you, so you must know why I'm here then."

"No specifics, but you give me the impression of someone who trusts his intuitions, so the choice here, Frank, is that what you call a whim is actually a wish to see those instincts through. Am I totally off the mark?"

"No, you're right. Of course, I didn't expect less of you. I knew, the moment we faced each other this morning, that I was in the presence of a rather evolved female—honestly, I felt naked."

"You see, Frank, I kind of sensed you had me all figured out—why I liked you on the spot. By then I had already made up my mind about connecting for a closer look at you."

"Feel free to probe, I won't pretend I can prevent you from doing so. But remember, you might expose something you may not want to share."

"Fair enough, but I trust my skills of secrecy. Don't you have any of your own?"

"Sure I do, but nothing pertaining to the two of us."

"Since you were eating by yourself when my friends and I had dinner last night, you must certainly have made an opinion of our gathering—that I'm interested in. Do you mind telling?"

"As you wish. The nine of you reminded me of a game that came to me in a dream, involving three groups of mismatched, identical objects—the point was to reunite those pieces into three distinct, powerful wholes."

Homura Oshiro faced me with a look that betrayed deep probing of my memory banks. Likely, she was foraging for veracity into my somewhat modified version of the truth.

"Sorry, I didn't expect your mind to be so colorful, Frank—a dream you say? That is most peculiar. I would never have imagined someone would come up with such an answer to my question. You're either extremely creative or I'm mistaken about you— whichever way, 'liking you' is understating it!"

— o —

Homura Oshiro's body was one of nature's works of art. She was also a fun and resourceful lover, but nothing over the top. She was my kind of woman—not like Jillian was—but one that belonged to an alternate version of my life, a side unexplored perhaps. If the mind had pulled us towards the rapids, the probing of carnal depths had ushered us back towards our point of balance. I fully let go, free of the tinge of apprehension that had been with me since Klaus Nussbaum left my apartment. If sweet Homura was dangerous, then I didn't mind dying in her arms, poisoned by the sting of her love.

She was gone when I woke up. I was glad to find myself alone in my room; not that I regretted what happened, but I preferred it when lovers had important things to do in their lives. The closeness came later, when nothing remained to challenge the trust.

But Homura Oshiro was definitely presenting an enigma of forbidden nature. I wasn't even sure how it was possible for the two of us to exist on the same plane of reality. I had traveled possibilities on a few occasions, entered portals into zones of existence that forcefully countered my presence—this one was sucking me in with the intension of not letting go. I was also attracted to it because it was in my nature to follow paths to their ends. No doubt I would see more of this delightful woman, but not at the resort—we were done here—Vancouver likely. Her card was slipped under my watch; I instinctively brought it to my nose—it smelled like her body.

— o —

I knew the group had left. It was felt like the aftermath of a happening, a vacuous kind of quality both serene and sad in almost a good way, or more precisely, like a form of release. Still no feds in spite of the Tesla waiting in the lot; it wasn't any of my business anyway. The skies were packing with clouds. I got into the Jeep and headed back to Clark's house.

——— o ———

# 5 – DEEPAN & EIKO

I laid the three amber sets back on the kitchen table. Which of the pieces was Homura Oshiro? I wasn't sure how I came to think I had found her, but one of the pyramids seemed to resonate at the same frequency the woman in my bed did last night. It was one of the three light pieces. I made it the primary for that group which I named *number one*. I placed the sets back with Homura's card in the Pelican case, closed it, and stashed it away in a secure place. In due time, each of *the ambers* would find their name.

I called Nussbaum on the scrambler to enquire about the feds. What he knew or didn't about them would likely bring perspective into the mystery of their disappearance. As far as he was concerned, the bureau's involvement was very unlikely since the assignment's criminal elements were only secondary to my work.

"Please make sure you're sniffing the right tracks; that's all I'm at liberty to say. I'll call you back with what I get on those two!"

—— o ——

There was little doubt in my mind that the two in question had met an undesirable fate. But how did they know my name and the nature of the assignment? There was a disturbing crossing of lines that didn't add up in my book. Even the Tesla didn't make sense. Actually, much of the last two days existed in some kind of vacuum, starting with Mace and Gomez's arrival in town. After all, those guys pretty much appeared the way they vanished; not to mention the general carelessness of how they went at their job.

Nussbaum called back.

"Frank, you're sure we're dealing with feds and not the mob, because as far as the bureau's concerned, your guys don't exist."

"Trust me on that, the mob dresses better! No, they're feds alright—I would know and so would you. So, if I'm following you, the bureau isn't missing any agents either, right?"

"Right. In other words, they didn't send anyone your way. Lazarus C. Mace and Dano Gomez don't exist as a team, within or outside the bureau."

"If I get this straight, it means their disappearance or death is of no consequence..."

"Only if you insist, but it won't get you far. Just stick to your end where you're most likely going to find your answers. And by the way, you're on your own, Frank—sorry, no calls!"

That said it all. He didn't even wish me luck this time around. He seemed annoyed I didn't get the point when he gave me the assignment. In fact, he didn't give me anything save for *the ambers*—no instructions, no lead, no meaning. It was my assignment, my responsibility, and likely, my fate. I almost regretted having called him, but I needed something on the feds, or whatever they were. A vacuum, the nature of the non-existent, zip... all belonged to the other side of a coin in a display case, never turned; unless you reached in there and flipped it around. Got it! I felt a sudden urge to connect with Homura Oshiro.

— o —

"Of course, Frank, I'll be waiting for your arrival. I'm sorry I had to slip out, but I knew you'd understand— there was a change of plans. Call me when you get here."

I was relieved she took my suggestion to meet in Vancouver with the same anticipation that motivated my need to connect. I couldn't lie that I was attracted to her, but there existed a thread between us that couldn't be denied, an energy force beyond mind and flesh. I wanted to make sure I wasn't the only one feeling it.

In the meantime, I needed to verify the one thing that was still sticky about my stay at the resort. I called the Silver Lodge to connect with the bartender.

"Tilda speaking... Jeremy who?... Sorry, no Jeremy here... No, I don't remember you from two nights ago—too many customers—unless you spoke with me directly and left a lasting impression, but I don't recall it was the case. My co-worker's Sergio if you should know... Thanks, you as well!"

That settled it. My intuitions had taken me into the layers of their births and I was all the more enrobed in mystery from it. I was becoming aware of straddling realities, unless madness had taken hold on me. I could just as well have been a ranting fool on the streets, caught in the perpetual drama of illusion. Perhaps, to alien eyes, we were all such ranters. But it suited my character to have a foot in the unknown, providing said unknown was where my assignment bore its fruit.

— o —

Two non-existent feds, one vanishing bartender, a stay at a resort whose recorded events contradicted those of my experience and conclusions... a whole that defined an assignment that read like the denouement of a new and slanted life chapter. Who in the world paid Nussbaum so that I would find myself amid the vacuity of the last few days, and for what reason!? But as he said, the answers lay ahead, and apparently—deeper.

All the personal questioning made me queasy; I actually disliked it immensely. Best was to shut my mind and fall within the cushion of the moment where all the action I needed resided. I had established a link between my *ambers* and *The Nine*. There was a placement of extreme significance that had to be negotiated with acute caution. Two zones defined, one by objects, the other by humans. The crux was to bring light to where my assignment needed me to be, likely, somewhere in between. A place in the middle was OK by me; it sounded safe enough—like the eddy.

I didn't want anyone to stumble across *the ambers*, yet I had the strong feeling they needed to remain close to me. The Pelican case was small enough to fit in a travel backpack, I just had to keep it with me at all times—that simple. I threw my things in the front seat of my car, re-parked the Jeep in the garage, and drove onwards to British Columbia.

— o —

Depending on traffic, it was roughly a four-hour drive from Greenwater to downtown Vancouver. Homura Oshiro lived in a Coal Harbour high rise, off West Cordova and Jervis Mews. I was familiar enough with the city to know it was a pretty posh neighborhood and quite expensive. It appeared my wild acquaintance was wealthy; nothing I didn't expect, but it at least affirmed that business was good and resources aplenty.

I made the trip in good time and called my host as promised. She asked me to leave the car with the doorman and take the express elevator to the top floor. Security checked my credentials—all was in good order. The lift took me directly to the penthouse's secure lobby where Hans and the other bodyguard were stationed. They looked at me briefly, nodded, and opened the sliding armored door that led into the place. Homura welcomed me in, asking about the drive and whether I would prefer freshening up first or later.

"I presently have guests; it's up to you whether you wish to meet them or not. I figure you'd probably want to wash away those hours on the road."

"Perfect, I'd love that!"

"Feel free to join us on the terrace when you're done. You and they actually crossed paths when we left the restaurant at your lodge; they're business partners."

"Lovely, please let them know I'm looking forward to being introduced."

— o —

Before hitting the shower, I briefly glanced at the *Vancouver Sun* left on the foyer's entrance table. I wasn't quite prepared for the news of two dead Security agents discovered off a Crystal Mountain trail in Washington State. The cause of death remained to be named, but the authorities didn't rule out murder. I should have panicked, but instead, my foot in the unknown found solid ground—there was something familiar about it.

— o —

My host introduced her two guests: the Asian woman with the Mohawk as Eiko Kohno, and the elder gentleman of Indian descendance as Deepan Sharma.

Eiko: "A pleasure to make your acquaintance Mr. Marks, Homura spoke of you in lovely terms; you left an excellent impression."

Deepan: "It is my pleasure as well, Frank, nice to meet you; and yes, I remember you sitting by yourself in that awful restaurant, if I may say."

Homura: "Did you catch the news about the two dead bodies found outside the resort? That's quite shocking!"

"I just read about it; Security agents of all things! I came across them a couple of times before they vanished out of thin air. There was something offish about them, and for a minute I wondered if they weren't after me."

29

Deepan: "Why would you feel that way, Frank, you didn't do anything wrong, I hope?"

"Not that I can think of. As a matter of fact, I told Homura I ended up at the resort mostly on impulse. I was essentially killing time while I figured personal matters out."

"Maybe those matters led you there, Frank," Eiko responded, amused.

"Yes, there could be some truth to that by the way things stacked up."

Deepan: "We were aware of two gentlemen intent on bringing discomfort to our party the night we all merged at the restaurant; our escort took notice as they tried to follow us. So, you see, they appeared to have been on both of our tails, providing they were the same individuals, of course."

"There isn't a doubt they were, Deepan."

Eiko to me: "If that's the case, there are great chances that we all might be suspects in the eyes of the law, am I right, Frank?"

"I'm sure you're aware I should be last with the ability to answer your question, Eiko."

Deepan: "Frank isn't only right, he also handed you back your bait, Eiko. What do you say we all move past testing each other and enjoy the little time left before we leave?"

It was quick thinking on Deepan's part. Eiko was moving too fast and he sensed she was about to give too much too soon. It by no means came across as a weakness; it was simply her style to be surgical in seeking answers. At that point, I started to suspect the three females to be the primaries, hence why I picked Eiko as the main piece in my number-two set—notwithstanding that I still had to define which one of them offered sympathetic characteristics. As to Deepan, I needed the collective energy of all *the ambers* to ascertain his place. There was something ancient about him that urged me to be particularly cautious about the possibility of error. With that revelation, I found the root of my early apprehension about the assignment: I couldn't afford to be wrong—ever.

——— o ———

# 6 – NIGHT OUT

Homura Oshiro came straight to the point.

"I didn't forget our night spent together, Frank, and as much as my body desires the touch of yours, there are other important reasons why I asked you here, or if you prefer, why you made the choice to call."

"I believe we're on the same page, except you may know where I'm going, while I'm not so sure at my end. Do I make sense?"

"Perfectly. Although you may be wrong about how much I know—for that, you and I, as well as at least one of the others, must spend the time necessary to ascertain we're not mistaken about what we believe is our common interest."

"To be clear, Homura, my interest is still to be defined; I'm mostly working on intuition, following whatever shows up along my path."

"But you do recognize the callings as of significance to you, don't you?"

"I recognize you seeking to make contact with me as extremely significant, although I'm still unclear about the motives."

"Then we must define the nature of that significance to determine whether you and I are meant to work together or not. If yes, I believe you know more than you're willing to tell, which would be expected, if not highly desirable of you."

"Are you saying that you're contemplating the possibility of a better fit to the post?"

"No, I wouldn't quite put it that way; I'm talking about a skilled impostor passing as you, Frank."

"And now is the time at which you would unmask the villain, I suppose?"

"Perhaps, but at least I would be in position to form an opinion."

"And Hans and his friend out there would take care of the rest?"

"Well, by the sound of it, I'm inclined to think that you believe they murdered the agents. My advice to you, Frank, is that you recognize how the possibility of bad judgment could deeply impair your travels. We're not a criminal organization, so don't let your imagination spoil the little we have together."

"So, why the bodyguards?"

"On the other hand, there are criminal elements seeking what we have."

"In my defense, you cannot prevent me from forming opinions of my own, anymore than I can of yours."

"Do you really believe we killed those two men?"

"No."

"Then it's my turn to trust we're on the same page. I suggest we go out for dinner and some dancing thereafter—my treat of course!"

— o —

Homura picked a restaurant on Coal Harbour Quay, a short distance from the tower. It was an easy stroll along the boardwalk with just the right amount of sea breeze to invigorate the senses. Daylight had passed the torch to the flickering glitter of North Vancouver, as everywhere, the beautiful city awoke to the glow of neons and the rise of its notorious nightlife. Our table was ready for us, courtesy Homura's deft use of her cell phone before leaving. But then, as a reenactment of the close past, two feds in their thirties sat at the end of the large room, directly looking at us.

"You noticed?" I asked.

"Yeah, there're always two of them wherever I go in public, solo or with partners. We believe they have a pair on each of us when we're not together."

"And they know of your very moves every time you go out or travel somewhere, I presume?"

"Correct."

"I'm not a partner, yet the two dead ones were on me before I reached the resort; what do you make of it?"

"I believe you have something they may want as well; that's the reason why I connected with you—one of our informants caught them accosting you at the bar."

"You mean Jeremy the bartender? Is he stationed in Vancouver as well?"

"You move fast, Frank; looks like we're going to be past playing games in no time. Yes, Jeremy works for us."

"How did he manage to switch roles with Sergio, the regular guy, if you don't mind me asking?"

"He didn't; it was his real job."

"I get it; just give me some time to process the information—brain break, if you know what I mean."

"It's fully understandable, but I gather it's not your first time at this."

"Well, this one's a first, but I've been where few dare going, if that's what you mean."

"I understand this is a unique case—why we deemed you fit for the job, but I had to make sure since it was my responsibility to check you out."

"Was the sex, part of the checking?"

"Not required, but you looked like someone I could like, remember?" Homura teased, winking.

— o —

The feds followed our limo to the club. They were dressed exactly like Mace and Gomez and roughly of the same build. For an instant I flashed on the nightmare that all the pairs were clones driving white Teslas. When I shared my thoughts with Homura, she practically sighed, "They might as well be."

I had thought my companion might have liked to be the night's sensation—she had the looks, the energy, and the command—yet she stuck by me, avoiding the wild dancing for the intimacy of torch songs and body closeness. I thought about Jillian for a second; I knew she was there somehow, supportive as usual; that was her gift to me as she left our world. Homura looked me in the eyes, pensive. I wouldn't have been surprised if she had sensed my ex's brief presence.

"Your emotions betray the passage of time through much healing, Frank. Your losses have become your strongest assets. Gains only have short-term value, while what time takes from us never leaves."

"I wish I could be where that came from, Homura, it must be a magical place. I imagine one of serenity where the wisteria blooms."

"Then we are there together, Frank."

— o —

As the chauffeur drove us back to the tower, we leaned against each other, cushioned by the soft leather of luxury, taking in the present of this strange world in which we existed as temporary visitors. Beyond it lay the spheres of our eternal souls. That night, Vancouver was just that—a world in between Ms. Oshiro's and mine.

——— o ———

# 7 – AMBRUS DEME

It was the first rainy morning of the season. Vancouver was layered in shades of gray. From the height of the tower, the north part of the city, across the waters, lay low at the feet of giants. Homura and I didn't sleep together—didn't wish to. Maybe our bodies did, but there was a line of responsibility that couldn't be crossed—not until we were clear on the terms of our collaboration. There was an important member my host insisted I meet before laying down the cards on the table. His name was Ambrus Deme, a man of Hungarian parentage, who, as the rest of *The Nine*, resided in Vancouver. Homura stood looking out the glass sliding doors, her naked body revealed in a play of light through the delicate fabric of her gown. Out of the sensuality of the moment, arose a longing for something lost in distant times, memories I could no longer reach—as if the past I was familiar with overshadowed another. She turned around.

"I'm sorry you didn't sleep well, Frank, but didn't the night unveil new truths or doubts about us?"

"Truths and doubts are all the same to me, Homura, they're only perceptual markers along the path of defining identity, purpose, and the nature of consciousness."

"What I implied was, 'Do you still want to go on with it?' You understand what is being asked of you, right? Your life will never be the same whether you succeed or fail in reaching the end of your travels; meaning what you refer to as your assignment—am I being clear?"

"Stopping now would be nothing more than the failure you speak of. Starting with meeting you, I realized my life would never be the same. I understood then that the assignment was serving two purposes, a personal one and the one of your group; or *The Nine* as I've come to think of you guys."

"And before meeting me, you were just on a case, nothing personal, correct?"

I had to think about the question for a moment.

"Well, I called it an inverted assignment from the get-go, mainly because it felt like it moved counter to what I had been accustomed to—but not necessarily a life changer. I was intrigued, but not irreversibly drawn to it."

"My role was to make contact with the investigator picked for the case—it's definitely a case at our end—but I had never envisioned that he would be intrinsically tied to it. In some respect, I'm in the same position as yours, where I find myself drawn to the Frank mystery, lost for words as to the nature of that attraction."

"That sounds complicated, but I have a solution for this kind of situation; it's called 'surrender.'"

"A case for *The Nine*—I like the name—becomes a quest for Homura. The only member who might have knowledge of this is Ambrus; he's the one who established contact with your agency. As to surrendering, I trust it's no longer too early."

With that, we made love till midday, both getting closer to our forgotten past via the channels of pleasure and sating. When we were done, we stood naked under the light rain that played the objects of the terrace in minute rhythmic tones. It was cold, but we didn't care. We faced the world before us—the one in between. Indeed, nothing would ever be the same.

— o —

Ambrus Deme was in his early sixties, but aside from his graying cropped hair, he radiated the energy of a much younger person, while his appearance was one of a trained athlete. To say the least, his personality formed an impressive presence.

Ambrus: "Ms. Oshiro and I were the only ones in the group aware of you at the resort, for the simple reason the others haven't been told about this. It's a pleasure to have you here; even more so now that you have a personal interest in being on the case. The one thing Homura isn't aware of is the set you have been put in charge of. I encourage the two of you to share what you haven't told each other, while at the same time, I praise you for having exercised caution. To get to the point, I have long suspected an irregularity within the group. You see, we came together in pretty much the same way you are being introduced to us—we had never met before. By your sustained presence here, I'm assured you're aware we exist in a world independent from yours, and that this is merely a meeting ground, one that is known to us as *the median lane*, by which one naturally understands that crossing over is not only prohibited, but regarded as impossible. That being said, I'm in a position to believe that there is an organization on our side that is intent on challenging both law and physics. The severity of the matter lies in my suspicion of one of our members belonging to that organization—an impostor, if you wish. But because of the way we came to be, we are in no place to establish if a substitution was made or, in the worst case scenario, if said intruder wasn't simply the brain behind forming the group as a means to furthering their agenda. I have no doubt this may appear convoluted, but you have time and resources at your disposal to see your assignment through, and I hope it will bring you closer to a better understanding of the reasons why you should find yourself working with us."

"It may help if you were willing to tell me what your group does or represents."

Homura: "I'm at liberty to explain that to you as part of the sharing."

Ambrus: "So, we are done here for the time being. Welcome, Mr. Marks!"

He shook my hand energetically, hugged Homura, and aimed for the elevator without looking back.

—— o ——

# 8 – CENTRAL GOVERNMENT

I took the case containing *the ambers* out of my pack and set it on a low, black, polished concrete table, the only piece of furniture in the dedicated tearoom.

"Do you know what this is?" I asked Homura before opening it.

"I wasn't briefed on you being in possession of something of ours, so no."

I took the three boxes out, put them on the smooth surface, and asked again. She looked fixedly at them.

"How could it be? They're *ambers*, aren't they?"
"They are, and do you know what they do?"
"Enough of this, Frank, please take them out!"

She came closer, refraining from touching them, as if forbidden. There was a ritualistic aura to her demeanor that betrayed unmistakable awe of the pieces, as well as of my person.

"I know what they represent and I'm stupefied they were handed over to you. The one who bestowed upon you the honor of being their trustee, already knew you were the right person for the job; that I don't doubt! Now I realize the two of us meeting was all planned, although it appears Ambrus took great chances, which can only highlight the direness of our situation."
"He could always have taken them back."

"Of course, but I don't think he had the intention to. He trusted they would lead you to us, and that you'd know what to do with them."

"I do, but I'm without a clue as to why I was chosen—I'm just an investigator. How would you proceed if you were in my shoes, Homura?"

"I'm not at liberty to answer your question; it's an abstraction. Only the bearer knows. These *ambers* convey many meanings dependent on purpose, but only in the hands of capable interpreters. I'd never have imagined such a person wouldn't be from my world; it's not even conceivable, yet here you are. At this point, I'm not sure if I'm worthy of you. Your position is one of elevated status; you're practically untouchable."

"OK, Homura, you're overreacting; it's just a job! Please, allow me to explain what I've arrived at."

"Before you do, I'd like to tell you what I know. Each piece stands for one of our group. The context in which the main set may be deciphered and arranged, presets the path of its behavior. Only the reader, in this case, you, can identify the members in each of the triads. But situations, being unique, dictate which and who belongs where—it's never the same."

"I gathered as much. My role, as I understand it, is to put order to the set, while matching energies. I've come to the natural conclusion that the females, the lighter *ambers*, are the triads' fixed primaries—only the males move around. My job is to determine were those go. For now, I only have you and Eiko figured out. I'll reflect before matching Deepan to his *amber*, and of course, Ambrus will come next."

"Providing we have context, you still must know the questions in order to do that, I don't get it?"

"Apparently, neither context nor questions came first. And by the way, no room for error—game's over if I screw up!"

"I'm aware of that, Frank, but I'm glad your spirits are up. On the downside, I wouldn't know where to start in assisting you."

"You might have to improvise. In the meantime you could always give me the name of the third woman, so that I can assign her to the light *amber* of box three. Of course, I still have to meet her to ascertain the frequency."

"Her name's Aurora; she doesn't use a surname. Just curious—how did you find me?"

"That was easy; I fell in love with that *amber*."

— o —

We had dinner at home. Neither of us felt the urge to be distracted by entertainment, or the oppressive presence of the feds. According to Homura, there was too much at stakes, which became clear when she stunned me with the information that *The Nine* wasn't in fact a business group, but the governmental core of a country not totally unlike the United States.

"Asians, Indians, whites—no blacks or natives?"

"Different history, Frank—no slavery. The natives have their own governments, cities, and social structures."

"OK, how can you govern from Vancouver?"

"Who told you Vancouver isn't where we have our central government? Frank, nothing is as it seems. Don't forget what Ambrus said, this *is the median lane*, which is meant to look a lot like your world. It will change based on your skills of adaptation."

"Are you saying that our respective perceptions of this place are dissimilar?"

"Interesting—are you saying it isn't the case in your world?"

I had to pause to absorb the concept.

"Well, I guess the truth is in the eye of the beholder, as we say; it's a measure of philosophical reach."

"Philosophy is only the means by which we romanticize the unknown. We have long accepted that wide variances in perception are necessary to the expansion of collective consciousness. But you need to be updated on the reality of our two worlds: ours is far more advanced than yours on many levels, and our time travels towards your past. *The median lane* is neutral.

— o —

It promised to be a long education. In the meantime, I was disconcerted by my inaptitude to find Deepan's *amber*. The *sub-genetics* put him among the darker ones, but none of them became alive when I tried to make a match. It was too early in the game to cry foul play; if anything, it focused my attention on the trickery of the assignment—that of navigating logical thinking against the grain of deception. According to Ambrus, Deepan wasn't aware of the specifics of my job, or that I was in possession of the *ambers*; therefore, there weren't any reasons for him to shield his person. What was obvious about the gentleman was his countenance—the reflection of his status as an elder member. Of course, each of them had to have been selected on aptitude, but based on loose intuition, he appeared particularly suited for the post. Maybe he didn't belong to any of the triads, except as a continuously moving energy. That was a thought! I turned to Homura.

"Does Deepan befit any elevated status within the group?"

"Yes, he's the president, the only one with a public profile. Technically, we're all on a par, but we can't confuse the citizenry with a political hydra. In our eyes, he's simply the sacrificial lamb."

"Wow, I get it. I assume you're not talking about a cabinet here?"

"No, we, as a whole, are *the* president—Deepan's the protruding head."

"Why only three women, and Asian for that matter?"

"We represent demographics, not genders. We don't need to make a point about sexes—only about dominant characteristics you may not be in position to comprehend. Why ask when you wisely discovered we're the primaries?"

"I guess I'll catch up with the details. So, back to the point: could it be the reason why I'm about to conclude that Deepan's *amber* is in a constant state of flux between triads?"

"Just tell me when you're sure—I'll approve of your discovery then."

Never an easy answer, but I was onto something; it was just a matter of slowing down my thoughts and home on the right frequency. But honestly, nothing could have been done without Homura around. I just had to avoid muddying the narrative with irrelevance. We had to firm up as a team. For now, she was in some kind of funk about the implications of a coup within the group, actions bound to savage the fundamental makeup of government in her country.

"More questions if you don't mind, Homura."

"Go ahead, I'm here for them."

"About the feds, why would they go after government?"

"They don't; they're either from Secret Service or Security. They're around to protect us, not harass us as Deepan insinuated. It's an inside joke; they create discomfort at worst. That's why the death of the two at the resort highlight how close we are to a catastrophe—the impostor is getting bolder and perhaps desperate."

"Alright, this may sound naive, but can't any of you sense who the culprit might be?"

"Frank, you must understand that except for Ambrus and me, nobody's aware of the possibility of usurpation. They wouldn't know!"

"How did Ambrus find out?"

"He was head of Security in the two previous administrations—he has his sources. That's all I know."

"OK, and hopefully last for now, who chooses the members of *The Nine*?"

"It's a lottery. Applicants must have special aptitudes, experience, and a clean bill of health. Aside from that, the formula remains the same: three females, six males, three colors."

"Who's in charge of the lottery; doesn't it sound a tinge dystopian to you?"

"Dystopian is an unfair adjective for a socially sound world, Frank. People have long recognized that Artificial Intelligence is better suited than humans when it comes to making rational choices in appointing government, so they voted for intelligent machines to take over the task. It turned out to be a very wise decision."

"Very interesting—what about political parties; don't you have any?"

"No—*The Nine* has made their need obsolete."

Pending further interaction with Ambrus, Homura and I were on our own, with a clueless me at the helm of a rudderless assignment.

———— o ————

# 9 – POST-MEETING PARTY

I made it clear with Homura that I wouldn't accept any nonsense about the statuses of *amber* bearers. Honestly, I was being put off by it; plus *untouchable* meant something entirely different in my world. I wanted the classic Ms. Oshiro back, the exceptional woman I had deemed far ahead of the pack, back at the resort. She understood, admitting to a moment of weakness occasioned by a sense of disorientation around *The Nine's* misfortune. I expressed my sympathy for her pain, but I knew I had lacked in the tact department when she responded by asking me to be gentle on her and to exercise due patience. My carelessness was put to shame by the firmness of her words. I apologized.

— o —

There were one woman and four men I hadn't met yet, all without any knowledge of the case. I could only be introduced to them as a close acquaintance of Homura's, but lying was out of question; they were much too witty for lies. Anyway, I still had to find Deepan and Ambrus among the amber figures. There was one last particularity pertaining to the set I hadn't enquired about yet: the insects trapped inside the petrified resin. When I brought it to Homura, she was surprised I hadn't asked, since it was the most striking part about the pieces.

"If you look closely, their shapes, postures, and sizes are supposed to give you clues about their counterparts. But since I've never been chosen as a reader, no-one in the team ever is, I can't specify. It's up to you to bring your interpretation to a conclusive end."

— o —

I should have heeded the detail earlier. I found Ambrus's *amber*, a mid-toned one, with a combination of instinct and logic. The two vibrated at reasonably close frequencies (the instinctual part) and upon observing the insect, the largest of the group, I came to the conclusion, with the help of my earlier observations, that only *he* could have befitted the size. Finally, since the case dictated placement and he and Homura were the only two to have been on it, he had to belong with her in the *number one* triad. I entered the information to the list.

As to Deepan, I temporarily assigned him a spot by Eiko in *number two*, even though his *amber* was still to be found. After all, Homura introduced them to me as a pair. I understood it didn't add up to much.

— o —

My thoughtful partner figured that a meeting followed by a party was the best way for me to get close to the remaining of *The Nine*. The murder of the two federal agents was the chosen topic to be discussed since it was close to home—not a chance to have it voted down. The party, on the other hand, was when I came in as Homura's friend, and where I would be free to roam. It was arranged for the first half of the event to happen in a little-known, secluded room of *Five Masts*, a starred

49

restaurant within walking distance of the tower. The party was set to follow at Homura's penthouse.

My role was to welcome the early guests, namely wives, relatives, and close friends, until the return of the group from the meeting; although Homura insisted that I accompany her on her walk to the restaurant.

Then something happened.

Halfway to the place, a survival instinct alerted me to an irregularity in our surroundings. Without thinking, I pushed Homura to the ground as a number of shots were heard: a flurry aimed at me barely missing my head, and several from the feds that failed at bringing the assassin down. Homura leaped as if ready for battle, but it was over. We looked towards the empty space left by the shooter, both of us acutely alert, positively unshaken, and irrevocably resolute to protect each other. The agents stayed behind, scanning for other potential dangers, but none were found. We resumed with our walk as if nothing had happened, even though everything had changed. It was obvious someone wanted Frank Marks dead.

— o —

Homura called Hans from the restaurant; she wanted him to pick me up in the armored Mercedes reserved for such occasions. I tried to refuse, but she wanted nothing of it.

"Go back there; not a word will be mentioned at the meeting. I have no doubt the attack is connected to your assignment, so I guess Ambrus and I are no longer the only ones to know about the case. The impostor has people on the outside, and I wouldn't be surprised if the murder of the two agents at the resort was intended to inculpate you. Please, return to my place to take care of the guests. It's only a two-hour meeting; I'll leave immediately after it."

— o —

I was first drawn to Aurora whose energy matched my chosen *amber* to a T. She was funny in a way only a free spirit could be, mostly by approaching all subjects of conversation from a witty slant in the narrative. She was personable—the ideal quick friend—but without the flightiness of character often associated with social butterflies. We were joined by Frederick Karpf, a man in his fifties, single and gay. As all the others, he was extremely fit, although he couldn't have been taller than five-six. Still, he was a commanding presence worthy of the respect demanded by his position. Unlike Aurora, my answer to his, "How do you know Ms. Oshiro?" was briefly the object of scrutiny, until Deepan intervened by putting his arm around my shoulders and asking jovially, "How's Frank Marks, doing today?"

Frederick: "I wasn't aware you two knew each other, I apologize for my indiscretion."

Aurora: "Always the suspicious kind when it comes to meeting new people; no wonder you can't find a suitable partner."

Frederick: "I would take offense coming from anyone else, but as you probably don't know yet, Frank, our dear friend here has been lamenting to me about the loneliness in her heart for such a long time, that I even contemplated becoming straight so that I could come to her rescue."

Deepan: "Well, Frank, as you know, there's no price for candor—what better way to get acquainted to new faces! But I almost forgot I was looking for Eiko—enjoy!"

Frederick: "Looks like Deepan's in top spirits tonight, not what I'd expected after such a dark meeting."

Aurora: "People compensate in weird ways."

— o —

Aurora's was a given, while Karpf had exposed enough facets to keep me from forming a conclusive opinion of his person. By his intervention, Deepan had highlighted why he befitted the role of the constant mover tentatively bestowed upon him. Until further notice, he didn't belong to any triad, although in his rotation, he forced another player out of a regular spot, creating more movers in the process. I sensed crumbling logic below the concept. The distinct possibility I was interpreting this all wrong showed its ugly head. Did Deepan know more than I was told? Surely, his interruption during Karpf's scrutiny was out of character for someone with lesser perspective. He could only have been trying to protect me—if not from the man himself, from the potential of infectious suspicion within *The Nine*.

I left Aurora and Frederick, to join Homura who stood alone. She smiled the way a true accomplice smiled, with a special spark in her eye. I sensed in her a deep wish to have her space back to herself, for the party to be over with, so that she could let her feelings go free to explore the multiplicity of scenarios that were rising from a dangerously close unknown.

"Feeling like we're wasting time by allowing this party to go on?"

"Yes, but I also know that patience is our strongest ally. You and I have a lot on our plate, haven't we?"

"Knowing that the villain is in the room, free to roam amongst the props of the ordinary, all powerful while we stand paralyzed in our blindness, is what gets to me the most, dear one."

"I'm glad for your eloquence—it's a measure of your strength—it inspires trust in you."

"Much appreciated. Deepan is proving to be an ally; is there something I still should know about him?"

"Being the head makes him a better overseer. I'm certain he's not involved in the case, but I wouldn't be surprised if he intuitively knew what's going on. After all, any guest from across the neutral zone betrays exceptional circumstances, yet he didn't flinch at your presence. Eiko also sensed something out of the ordinary, but she prefers to get her own answers. So, don't be surprised if she were to connect with you."

"Thanks for the heads up; I'm prepared. In the meantime I still have to be introduced to the last three members."

"Let me walk you around then; I see Suneet Kumar isn't busy. He's one of our elders, as are our other two Indian members. He also may be inquisitive as to your presence among us."

"Any special strategy?"

"Tell him the truth without mentioning the case; I'll take care of the rest."

Suneet Kumar was a very fit, smartly-dressed septuagenarian, whose stance would reduce pretense to dust if he didn't know how to avoid such encounters. Massive knowledge was apparent below the aura of dignified pride surrounding his person. He could also be a charming gentleman.

"My pleasure, Mr. Marks. You look familiar; have we met before?"

"We passed each other briefly last week at the Crystal Mountain resort. You and I were dining at the same restaurant."

"I see. But why weren't we introduced then?"

"We couldn't because I hadn't met Ms. Oshiro yet."

"I see, a new friend. I'm sure Homura here was intent on letting us know?"

"Yes, Suneet, a very new friend and an important one at that."

Suneet: "Is it the fact he's from the other side that makes him important, or that he should find himself among us without so much as an official background check requiring approval of the group?"

Homura: "Then I must remind you that approval isn't required for soul mates. It's an indubitable part of social standing that applies to government as well."

Suneet: "Indeed, my apologies, my dear; it is of course also part of the inherent trust between us. We all still are a bit shaken by the news of the murders."

"No issue, these are testing times."

Suneet: "They truly are, Homura, but to our friend: a pleasure meeting you—may I call you Frank?"

"Absolutely—the honor is mine, Suneet."

— o —

"Well, that wasn't so hard." Homura remarked.

"Soul mates, eh?"

"Was it a total lie, Frank?"

"Obviously, he believed you, so I guess not."

"What I mean is, was it inappropriate?"

"Homura, I'm afraid of the term, that's all. I once had a soul mate who I think is still with me in spirit. But she died on assignment, shot on the street like I almost was today. It's a bit too close to home for me right now. In the meantime, I'm not denying that we may have a deep heart connection. I do indeed feel love for you, you know that?"

"When I said I trusted you, I meant intimately as well. That's enough for me to honor what I told Suneet."

"Trust and love bring us halfway there; resilience through time will take us to the finish."

"There's the wind of promise in your words; can I depend on it?"

"I can't promise I won't be shot at again; aside from that it's safe to say we're in it for the long run."

— o —

Lionel Watts stood by the edge of the terrace, looking across the Vancouver Harbour waters. Slightly heavier-set than the other men in the group, he conveyed the stance of a regimented weight-lifter hooked on power protein smoothies. He could easily have been mistaken for one of the bodyguards. I moved to his right, introducing myself as the stranger in the party.

"Frank Marks—Homura's friend from across *the median lane*. I figured it was a good time to mess with the serenity of the moment," I humored.

He turned sideways, sizing up the opponent in me before relaxing and shaking my hand.

"Yes, of course, Frank; I think it was Eiko who spoke of you in one of our gossip groups—Lionel Watts, Lionel for short."

"Any conspiracy theory regarding my person lately?"

"I like a man of humor, Frank, but in all sincerity, you've got to understand that we're all a bit curious about new friends. Personally, I prefer open crowds to inbred ones, so I welcome you among us. When all fails, time remains the ultimate indicator of who's to trust and who's not. I always start with trust before making my way to the truth."

"I respect a man of wise words. I just thought I'd say hi—great meeting you, Lionel!"

"See you around, Frank!"

— o —

In spite of a few hiccups, all went well. But before I got a chance to meet the last of *The Nine*, he and his wife had left the party. His name was Ray Anand, another septuagenarian of good breed and manners, according to Homura.

"I will invite him and his charming wife in the next few days for dinner, so you'll have plenty of time to record the frequency at which he resonates," she humored.

"Thanks! Looks like the party's over; I'm tired and I wouldn't mind sharing a bed tonight."

"You got it, Frank; I can't wait to wrap myself around you and forget about the world."

———— o ————

# 10 – OUT WITH EIKO

The morning following the party, I retreated to the serenity of the tearoom, *the ambers* lined up on the dark, polished stone-like surface in the order they were given to me. I set the list and a few notes next to them—the task was to put names on the remaining five. I had Homura and Ambrus in triad one; Eiko and an impermanent Deepan in two; and last, Aurora in three. But first, I needed to firm up Deepan's position. By changing places, he not only was displacing the other two elders, but making *the ambers* in that color group impossible to identify. It made sense at the level of their collective status as the wise men in the group, but as I said before, it challenged the logic of them belonging to any of the triads. My number one theory was losing steam.

The other option was that Deepan indeed belonged with Eiko, meaning that the difficulty in identifying his *amber* lay in the nagging obvious of items too familiar to see. Of course, I had to be cautious to not let my thinking be influenced by untimely suspicion. My lack of familiarity with the elements of the case worked against me at the logical end. What was required of me wasn't my brain, but the unlocking of memories that, somehow, had brought me to this room.

It came to me that I needed Eiko to get to Deepan; there was a symbiosis between them that could potentially hold the key in charge of the door to his inner workings. After all, I had enough of a sense that the primary was the connecting link between the two males in each triad. At that very moment, I felt released from paralysis by the forces of revelation. The three females were the immutable parts, while the males switched places on a per case basis. I needed to lock myself into my assignment in order to reach the level of clarity required to identify *the ambers*. For that, I had to accept that I was an intrinsic part of it, not just an outsider anymore.

There had been too much thinking, useless rationalizations, and not enough immersion in the present. I closed my eyes and entered the neutral space of private meditation. When I returned from it, I placed the three darker figures in a line, facing the lighter ones. Nothing happened. On my second try, I hit a home run; all three elders came alive with a glow—I had a match. I isolated the pairs in order to identify each of the darker *ambers*. Deepan Sharma, as I had anticipated, belonged to triad two; Suneet Kumar's *vibrational* energy was so tied to Aurora's that it practically created a line of blue light between the two, which prompted me to heed Klaus Nussbaum's words of caution: "They're shuffled for safety." Ray Anand, the only member I hadn't met yet, was left as the no-brainer who belonged with Homura. In the end, I didn't need Eiko to get to Deepan, and the elders' rotation was nothing but a measure of their placement as farthest from the primaries; which left me to deal with Fredrick Karpf and Lionel Watts.

— o —

I didn't realize hours had passed since I entered the tearoom. While on my break, I reenacted the shooting on the previous day's walk. It wasn't hard to imagine a beeline from our impostor to me. I was an undesirable element in their plan, unless I was desirable as a dead man. After all, the reason I hadn't been apprehended for the murder of the two feds while on *the median lane*, was only because I was presently on the inside, a position which reversely made me extremely vulnerable to someone in *The Nine* with an agenda to protect.

— o —

Eiko and Aurora's *ambers* were paired to the last two—those associated with Fredrick Karpf and Lionel Watts. Only one came alive, meaning Ambrus was in the wrong triad. I added Homura to the lineup and shuffled the three males—two responded, in the process of which I lost Ambrus to the enigma of the unresponsive one. I was wrong to have relied on an approximate energy reading linking him to Homura on the merit of both being the only ones involved with the case—maybe Deepan was onto something after all. That left me with the villain hidden among the mid-toned amber pyramids, and no names. I was time to enter a new layer of the case.

— o —

When I left the tearoom to join Homura in her study, I was met by Eiko who was coming out of one of the bathrooms.

"Hello, Frank, how did you enjoy the party?"
"Hi, Eiko, busy getting to know the group—why I didn't connect with you, I guess. What about you?"

60

"Just another party in the name of diplomacy; we're known to use posturing as a means to make ourselves important."

"I wouldn't have guessed it'd be the case; you all seem to be rather down-to-earth. Is there something I'm supposed to be reading in your words?"

"The right answer deserves an accolade; you're right, Frank, we're not that flighty. You may call it an introduction to Eiko Kohno. But tell me, weren't the meeting and the party just an excuse for you to meet all of us in the shortest time possible; isn't there something I should know?"

"I'm glad to observe that my early impression of you as a surgical investigator was correct. That being said, I will answer your question only under the umbrella of strict confidentiality. It's evident that you're aware my presence here is not just accidental, but I hope your interests are far removed from suspicion or mere curiosity—you're going to have to prove that first. Otherwise, this encounter has never happened."

"I could have you in deep trouble for this."

"I'm afraid you can't afford it; it's beyond the scope of your personal powers. Try it if you don't believe me."

"You're either a fearless bluffer or you mean it— either way, there's bound to be action, and action's my game. What do you say to that?"

"I say Eiko wants to know what I have."

"Just give me a fucking cue, Frank!"

"Alright, what about 'your house needs cleaning,' primary Kohno!"

"OK, you got my attention. Are you free to meet me outside in the West End? I have my fave hangouts there. I prefer to talk serious politics within the relative safety of my comfort zone."

"Any idea on how to lose the feds?"

"Depends whether they're with you or after you."

"They haven't arrested me yet."

"Then you won't be able to get rid of them—better get used to it. Eight o'clock at the Palm Leaf on Benman."

— o —

Homura came out of the study just as Eiko was leaving.

"Something I missed?"

"We're meeting later for a chat; it's personal."

"Sounds good; see you, Eiko!"

— o —

"So, Frank, any news about *the ambers*?"

"Some good, some not so."

"Can you clarify?"

"It appears our bad guy hides amid the mid-tone ones. One of them remains unresponsive, meaning Ambrus lost his place in your triad. Your connection to the case doesn't substantiate his position anymore; on top of it I must have misread his energy field. Now I can't put a name on any of the three, in spite of two matches to their respective primaries."

"But all you have to do is name these two, right?"

"Yeah, it shouldn't take me too long."

"So, what's the deal with Eiko?"

"You're gonna have to trust me on that; I need to take her into the confidentiality of the case, we need another ally. I know we can rely on her."

"I was wondering when you'd start taking charge. I love Eiko; I'm glad you made the choice."

— o —

Eiko was a warrior, petite with stealthy fluidity in her sinuous moves. Psychologically, she preyed on the weakness of man. She tolerated no bullshit, demanded quick answers, and savaged those who dared waste her time. What attracted her to me was the potential for a hunt. She knew what I meant by house-cleaning and it sure wasn't dusting the mantle. Somehow, she had smelled a rat and wanted part of the chase. She was unique among *The Nine* in that she belonged more to a punk band than she did to the highest echelons of government. But that was the beauty of the group, it covered the entire three-sixty of the sociopolitical field— no parties, no left, no right, no nonsense.

"You tell me that Amb, based on his sources as past head of National Security, put a case together, got in touch with your agency, and asked Homura to establish contact with you for the purpose of purging the group of a bad seed—that I get! What I don't is why you, a man who shouldn't even be breathing our air?"

"Nice—I've asked myself the same question, only to come to the conclusion that I didn't have a choice even if on some weird level I was drawn to the assignment for personal but obscure reasons."

"I dig the answer, man, but what about the set?"

63

"You know what it is and what it does; it was handed over to me to assist in my search, although I was warned that there would be dire consequences if I used poor judgment."

"No shit, someone forgot to mention it's a time bomb only the ultra-skilled can diffuse. Those guys are rock stars nobody can touch—you don't appear to be one of them though."

"Maybe your rock stars were indisposed and I got the call instead, so I'm here to accomplish what I'm being asked to do, and follow my heart wherever it leads me."

"You've got balls, Frank, but I think I could like you after all."

Eiko smiled and looked me in the eyes for the first time. It appeared a figment of trust had seen the light.

"I tell you what; you make copies of that list and your notes for me to study, and I'll get back to you with my thoughts. I know that group from the bottom up, and if there's a usable irregularity in there, I'll find it."

———— o ————

# 11 – BODY BAG

I decided to walk the twenty or so blocks back to Homura's place to clear my thoughts. There was a steady drizzle, but I welcomed the touch of water. The feds remained with Eiko—I wasn't aware of any others on my tail. Homura would have been horrified by my choice of returning alone without protection, but not Eiko, who saw my decision as one of toughness, and I believed it turned her on. The absence of agents posed a perplexing issue in regard to the case: whoever the villain was, he had enough leverage to pull Security out to expose me to menace. I realized I was about to take the fight to the streets without a backup plan. Within seconds of the thought, Eiko was by my side, pushing me into the shadows of a lane.

"Let's get the fuck out of here, the feds have bailed out, and that means we're in trouble! You got a gun, Frank?"

"I do, but it's loaded with blanks."

"That won't help much, dude!"

"I know, but I have my reasons."

Two silencer shots ricocheted against metal within a few feet of us—the hit man was close—too close. We ran to the end of the lane, chased by fire, aiming left on Bidwell towards the alleys accessing the sports fields. We hid in the darkness of trees. Eiko called Homura who sent Hans and his partner Philip to the rescue. We waited, ready to leap at the first bit of movement coming our way.

Eiko was calm, like danger on its best behavior before the storm. I reminded her of the first time we met when she so properly addressed me as Mr. Marks.

"Oh, shut up, Frank, I'm a diplomat, remember? I never show my true self on a first date."

"Got it—you're ready to claw this fucker if backup doesn't show up soon?"

"I'm so ready!"

Five muffled shots, three guns, and then nothing but the dragging of a body on gravel—it was all over for the assassin.

We joined Hans and Philip as they were stuffing the man into a body bag. No witnesses, no traces, save for some blood here and there in the wet dirt. It would be all gone by morning.

— o —

The bodyguards dropped me at the tower then drove Eiko back to her place. Homura was beyond herself in disbelief—I saw fury in her eyes. This time, the shooter had gone after one of *The Nine*, which was seen as unprecedented. The infiltrator's organization was on the move, ready to jeopardize government and send the country into chaos. Yet my job wasn't done, while alarming the group was likely to precipitate events towards a catastrophic end.

"What's the deal with the feds' vanishing act?"
"I don't know, Homura; they just weren't there."

"It would require an order from Security's highest levels to pull such a trick. I can see them not covering you, but in the case of Eiko, it's an unforgivable break in protocol."

"Well, as you can tell, our meeting was a successful mess. I like her style; nothing like the polite guest cozying up with Deepan on the day of my arrival—she's combat-ready."

"Actually, Frank, all of us are."

"I should have known by how fit you all are—but back to our shooting. As sinister as it sounds, with Eiko down, Security had all they needed to set me up for attempted murder."

"It's obvious someone wants you out of the picture, but to deem Eiko expandable is beyond reason."

"Then who in the group is the least likely to show sympathy towards her?"

"Her style makes her an easy target for dislike, so it's a toss between a few of the men. I'd say Frederick isn't too fond of her, mostly because he finds her manners brusque, to use his words."

"That hardly qualifies as a case of wanting her dead; what about something more visceral?"

"Nobody hates her, but I see how she could be seen as dangerous to an insider. Maybe your conversation was monitored—have you thought of the possibility?"

"Not since she guaranteed the place was safe."

"Now we know no place is safe anymore."

— o —

Before disposing of the body, Philip took thumbprints, various identification shots, and pictures of the gun. It was routine work among private security to sweep tracks with time and field-tested methods. Furnaces, concrete pours, and dog food processing plants were all parts of the reclaiming process. For some characters, even the past was reclaimed.

As it turned out, the hit man was an ex-Secret Service agent, which pointed in the direction of a rogue element in the agency—another nasty head emerging out of the foulness of bloated powers. The momentary absence of security was meant to create a window for the shooter. The reappearing feds could have simply said that by the time they reached Eiko, she was dead. After all, it wouldn't have been the first time she attempted to evade protection. She was the perfect prop for the bad guy to set me up as the killer, the ideal diversion away from festering malfeasance.

— o —

I hadn't reconnected with the amber set yet when Eiko called announcing she would be there in twenty minutes. Hans would pick her up, but she assured me that Security was back on track. Homura was gone for the day for a long meeting with an unnamed minister.

A business suit had replaced the leather. Eiko was back to being the diplomat, still surgical but with added coldness in case ice was required.

"I have something for you, Frank, are you ready to go over your list and notes?"
"Do you want to see the set?"

"No, that wouldn't help, I'm no psychic."

"Fancy some coffee; have you had breakfast yet?"

"I already had my vitamins, but coffee's fine. Are we certain this place isn't bugged?"

"I'm sure the guards outside have been on it."

"OK, Frank, assuming you have your placements right, we've still got three boys against the wall behind the glass, and we're relying on your skills of perception to identify the guilty one. One of the *ambers* doesn't react to any of the primaries, you say?"

"Correct."

"So, wouldn't it be logical if there actually was a disconnect at the human level—forget the appearances, I mean, a fundamental one?"

"That would be a given providing we could access those levels."

"You're ignoring the obvious, Frank, if we have an impostor, where's the guy who's supposed to be in his shoes?"

"I thought about it briefly, but the obvious is that he's not around for identification."

"Alright, let me rephrase it. You're an outsider given a window into our world via *the ambers*; if I were you, I would make it personal. Can't you guess where I'm getting at?"

"A bit far-fetched don't you think?"

"You're here, Frank, practically part of us; don't you get it? Hear it from the primaries: Homura's in love with you, I would die to kick out whoever's in my group to have you in there, and Aurora would grow the biggest crush of her life if she knew you had *the ambers*. You may not be the one, but you definitely make a good case for replacing the asshole in the group. Of course, we still need to explain why you ended up on the other side to start with.”

“Exactly, how can I erase my past? There are gems in there I would never think of parting with.”

“A visit to our world might give you a better perspective on how things work. The *median lane* is an alluring mix of both sides. As you experienced already, when you step off it, you’re left with memories that don’t connect with your normal reality—you either lose your mind or surrender. It’s different for us since we control the traffic. So, when we need to be here—as in now—it’s where we are. Homura originally thought she brought you among us, but I convinced her yesterday, before you and I got shot at, that you actually came of your own volition— you simply heeded the call. No-one from your side makes it here without ending up ranting on a street corner, but you look perfectly comfortable in this element. I would go as far as saying that you’re from our side, returning from a long journey, or some sort of detour.”

“I would be open to your suggestion if Jillian, my ex-partner, had never come into my life.”

“Don’t make an absolute out of a misconception, Frank, Jillian covered her assignment and moved on— you’re not going to find her back there—that’s all I can tell you in her regard.”

“I don’t get how you would know, but I came to understand that her death wasn’t a simple case of misidentification—it felt like there was something greater than both of us in it.”

“Good, you’re not so clueless after all.”

“So, what’s it like to be on the other side?”

“Probably not that different from here.”

“But here’s hardly any different from my end?”

"That's why it's called *the median lane*."

"I'm sure there's something I'm missing."

"Listen, Frank, whatever the details, you can't access our world, unless you're from it, anymore than we can show up in yours, unless we're from there—you get the nuance? What I'm saying is that if you're from our side and landed on the other, you're way ahead of the motherfucker who's trying to get us killed—am I losing you?"

"I can't say you aren't, but you make a convincing argument—how do we go about it?"

"You only had to ask!"

I couldn't say I didn't feel weird, but Eiko and I were still in the same room looking at Vancouver Harbour across the rain. There was a different quality to my environment I couldn't precisely describe, except in the form of a nuanced déja vu. I had been there before, not yesterday, but long ago. Eiko looked at me, amused.

"You see it's the same, just as I said."

"Save for a few excerpts of memory, perhaps?"

"Yes, those—it makes sense—you're from here, Frank!"

"So, what now?"

"We go back before anyone notices; we can't afford to let the cat out—not yet."

———— o ————

# 12 – THE IMPOSTOR

Even with a glimpse into the opposing traffic, I couldn't convince myself that it gave me a greater aperture into the case. In spite of Eiko's words, I lacked the conviction that I was an integral part of *The Nine*. I didn't doubt her—I doubted myself rather. Of course, the detour, as she called it, didn't conjure more than a theoretical notion, but I had to accept it as a plausible one nonetheless. More thoughts, more churning, more time wasted away from the main goal. One way or the other, if I didn't put names on those *ambers*, the case was toast.

Eiko had left and I was back in the tearoom, except this time the figures all seem to have a luminescence to them that I hadn't noticed before—all but one. I put it aside as to belonging to someone whose place had been usurped. Eiko's theory was off the charts, but I couldn't afford not to heed it; if it was my *amber*, I had to reclaim it, put my name to it, and place it in its allocated set. But I realized that for it to show itself, I would have to act the part—be the wild card in the team—I had no choice but to convince myself of it.

— o —

I was on a break when Homura returned. She looked drained from a combination of last night's action and her meeting with the minister. She told me that irregularities were found in other sectors as well, and that a number of whistleblowers had been found dead under dubious circumstances. She seemed to indicate that government was slipping from under *The Nine*. When I updated her on Eiko's input, her face brightened.

"I thought about it, Frank, especially after I spoke with her before you two left for your night out. It makes a lot of sense at our level, and I wouldn't be surprised if others in the group caught up with the idea."

"Our impostor as well, I gather."

"Which means that your life isn't just in danger; you're practically a walking dead. The feds aren't here to protect you, and likely, they won't be around for those too close to your person, meaning me as well."

"I'd say government is fully jeopardized."

"Yes, we must identify the suspect without delay. Is there anything I can do to help?"

"What about convincing me Eiko is right?"

"Focus, Frank, you're here, just as she said. What can be more convincing, besides, perhaps, hoping your ex lives among us?"

"That would do it for sure, but I'll take the light version."

"Go back to your childhood, Frank, all the way up to the point at which you and Jillian started working as a team. You met her at the agency right after you left your job at the bureau, am I correct? I suggest you look hard into how you met Klaus Nussbaum."

"I met him in Tacoma at a pub. He came in and sat next to me at the bar, asking if I had a light—the rest is history."

"What if I told you that pub never existed on your side, but only on ours and *the median lane*? Please don't ask me to prove it; we don't have time for that!"

"That wouldn't explain the past you're asking me to look into."

"You only have one past, Frank; you took it with you. You've been on assignment since then, essentially to prepare you for this. You and Jillian were the only ones to make the full crossing!

"Oh my poor mind, is this for real?! OK, let's say I should look for clues in my past—but why exactly?"

"Because there was once a young girl you fell in love with who was fond of you as well. Unfortunately, her parents didn't approve of the closeness and sent her away. We were both twelve."

— o —

The revelation struck me like lighting. Of course I remembered young Homura; I just had to be reminded of her! And Jillian from there as well! I didn't need proofs, everything made sense at once. I guessed Nussbaum was from there too; we never met outside *the median lane*— why he could hand the amber set over to me. The only mystery left was why Jillian and I ended up on the other side. Homura was quick to explain.

"You both were gifted with a rare genetic trait that immunized you from the dangers of crossing *the median lane*. You needed to be isolated from those interested in finding what made you different; you were just as useful to them, dead or alive. *The Nine* of the time deemed the other side relatively safe, although not safe enough since you could only connect with Klaus here, in the neutral zone where Jillian was shot. Somehow, you carried her back across so that her body couldn't be taken. It's likely

74

her murderers belong to our suspect's organization. Jillian was your twin sister; both of you were separated at birth. That's why your attraction to each other never took you into the throes of an all out sexual relationship—your genetic commonality prevented you to cross that line, but I have no doubt you came dangerously close."

"Damn, if this didn't convince me I'd be brain dead. It's war—time to find that son of a bitch!"

"The eight of us will be ready when you are; it's OUR war path, Frank!"

— o —

That *amber* was mine—period—all the more now that it glowed with Homura as its primary! Never mind when and how I got bumped off *The Nine*—that would come later—for now, I was a tick away from pulling the villain out of the three white males: Frederick Karpf, Lionel Watts, and Ambrus Deme. Of course, Ambrus was the odd man out; he initiated the case based on his long history at Security, deep access to its database, and knowledge of its inner workings. Yet, I hesitated naming him suspect number one because he was too frameable— something I learned from experience. I put him aside as unlikely. Two *ambers*, two suspects I briefly met at the party: Watts, who in spite of sizing me up upon introduction (mostly because I came out of nowhere), was solid and straight forward. I couldn't find a downside to his person. That left Karpf.

Frederick Karpf, if I remembered, was about to probe me when Deepan interfered. He wasn't doubtful—

75

just playacting the part. Aside from Aurora who was love-starved, and in search of affections she found in the man's purported understanding of the female nature through his personal choices in sex orientation, I didn't get the impression he was loved by the rest; although that detail came from Eiko's influence. There also was a strong possibility the gayness was a front. Perhaps it was just a bad case of profiling, but queen or stud, he had all it took to not be left loveless. Yet, he complained of his bad fortune, not at all concerned I was within earshot. There was a distinct blurriness to his person that undergirded my suspicion of concealment about his true identity. I analyzed the two trapped insects for clues—they looked complete and at peace—nothing blurry about them. Karpf became my number one suspect. All I was left to do was put Watts and Deme's names on the two remaining *ambers* by exposing them to Eiko and Aurora's primary energies. Both came to life, Ambrus to Eiko's and Lionel to Aurora's. I had finally located my suspect!

— o —

I immediately informed Homura, who took task of connecting privately with the remaining seven members for a secret emergency meeting without Karpf. She knew it had to be absolutely air-tight—no room for error—the traitor had to be neutralized before the news got to him!

We met the next day at an undisclosed location. Homura and Eiko facilitated while Ambrus and Deepan presided with the details of the case (which explained why the latter came to my rescue when Karpf was about to make trouble). Whether Karpf was in or out, *The Nine* faced a powerful organization by the name of *Adapted Control* that was deep in the process of deconstructing a government that took nearly a century to perfect. The only option left was to activate the team by arranging the three groups of *ambers* according to the order on my list. I had been urged to bring the set over. I took the pieces out of the boxes, formed three triangles of tetrahedrons which I grouped so that the three primaries touched each other. The whole set glowed until the room filled with a near-blinding orange iridescence. I asked for all to hold hands. The glow became us until it gently receded. We were one, we were armed, and the name of *The Nine* was voted in unanimously.

It was said that properly matched *ambers* amounted to a task force gifted with extreme powers. It was also said that a mismatch brought unprecedented ruin. I guessed I didn't do too badly. Now the time had come to face the man responsible for the murder of my beloved twin sister.

—— o ——

# 13 – ADAPTED CONTROL

A second emergency meeting with Frederick Karpf was arranged for the next afternoon at government headquarters. The purpose: to expose the man as a traitor and have him locked up. It required consensus, but the group was set to vote on his removal anyway. I wasn't permitted to join under existing protocol, at least not until asked in to testify and prove my identity as the denied member. The major issue for me was my mind, which wasn't quite ready to identify with my old self; not mentioning the myriad questions still unanswered that begged to understand how my history, on both sides of *the median lane*, was kept stitched into one past. To that, I was told my special skills were what saved it from coming apart, but the extent of the memory loss had been severe. Nothing time couldn't fix, though.

Slowly, I found myself in position to observe the differences between the two lanes. There was no central government building in the Vancouver of the world I had come from. My memories found their footing as I steadily gravitated towards my original reality. Things that were lost reconnected to their sources—the gap into which they had fallen had simply been born of two worlds made into one. I finally realized I had come home.

The building was surrounded by a tall wrought iron fence topped by arrays of cameras. It was where Deepan lived as official head of state—the visible part of *The Nine*. Armed guards controlled the main gates and all other entry and exit points, including underground emergency evacuation routes. I had been issued a temporary guest pass that allowed me to sit outside the meeting in the visitor hall. I remembered being there on several occasions as an agent when Ambrus was in charge of Security. As memory returned, my larger assignment began to take form—*Adapted Control* already posed a major threat when Jillian and I met through Nussbaum during the previous administration. In the back of my mind, I imagined we were meant to return together to save the day, which might have explained my sense of mild disorientation. But in what capacity was she to assist? Did she have her place in the group as well, and who replaced her? At that very moment, it came to me that she and I had been stalled; trapped to remain on the other side for much longer, if not forever. We should have returned before her death. Nussbaum must have known but chose to keep the information away from me. I felt reduced to a role in someone else's script, although, I doubted it hadn't been my choice all along to stay behind—I just wasn't remembering.

— o —

I had barely come out of my reverie when I perceived an increased Secret Service presence. It merely took a second before I realized I was he subject of their attention, and not Frederick Karpf. I remembered the floor plan of the building well enough from the early days to recall the concealed service door next to the bathrooms. I nonchalantly made my way to it while *Adapted Control* embedded forces awaited their orders. I was gone before they realized what had happened. In fact, more was

79

coming back into focus as my escape act took me to one of the emergency evacuation routes via an unguarded bypass. I emerged onto an unnamed subway terminal where a one-car train was on stand-by—the secret presidential line that connected with the main system via a second secret platform and a short series of corridors. I, for the occasion, managed to remember my old personal code which got the train going and gave me access to all the doors—it miraculously still worked. I counted on *The Nine* knowing what had happened as soon as the news of my getaway spread across all areas of Security. Sure enough, within minutes, Eiko called me on my cell to check on my whereabouts and give me the heads up. In the midst of the commotion, Karpf who had just been unveiled as an impostor, managed to slip out under the protection of the feds working for *A.C.*

"I'll pick you up at *Stadium* in ten; look forward to a bike ride!"
"In a business suit?!"

She didn't bother with an answer.

— o —

Eiko must have chosen the *Stadium-Chinatown* station based on how quickly she could get to me. Hopefully she was fast because I was there in no time, but so were *Adapted Control* at the end of the platform. I wasn't surprised to find Eiko clad in leather as she handed me my helmet. We left our pursuers behind in a one-wheel take-off, as two white sedans materialized behind us. But Ms. Kohno knew her way around the back lanes.

Soon, we were outside the city, out of reach, racing northbound on *Ninety-Nine*—destination unknown.

— o —

Emergency headquarters could only be accessed by active members, strictly on consensus. Frederick Karpf, by reason of his new status, was barred from it.

The *Aerie*, as it went, was considered the safest place for *The Nine* to regroup and take action. It was located in the town of Squaford, an hour's drive from Vancouver, inside a converted warehouse off the marina. It was one of a half-dozen sites prepared for such government emergencies, only known to specific, encrypted, and A.I. assisted computers.

Except for Ambrus Deme who stayed behind to consolidate a counteractive force to extract *Adapted Control* moles from the government, and Deepan Sharma as the head executive, all seven members and several bodyguards were now stationed in the retreat. *The Aerie* was essentially a control center for active leaders under pressure from outside forces, a place whence strategy and leadership came until hostilities were quelled.

Homura and I shared quarters. It had been difficult for the two of us to find solace in the love that we shared, but there would be time for it when things settled. For now, I needed to be updated on procedural details, as well as the nature and extent of the powers held by *the ambers*. But first, I yearned to be reacquainted with those I only had met briefly at the party, notwithstanding that I never was introduced to Ray Anand, the third elder. Ray's accommodations, as it turned out, were adjacent to ours, and thus we were given the opportunity to catch up right before settling in. He, as expected, was of athletic build in the style of gymnasts, muscular without the bulk, likely schooled in martial arts, with the addition of a keen intelligence backed by ample knowledge and insight. We instantly bonded.

— o —

Each of the individual quarters were laid out like standard two-bedroom apartments, save for the emphasis on security in the form of armored doors, high windows with bulletproof one-way glass panes, and computer systems protected by defense-grade hardware firewalls. Each was provided with an egress to the fire-proof underground control room, and access to the roof's helipad. I approved of the investment in protection.

Homura locked the door then turned around to give me a hug and rest her head on my shoulder.

"I wish it were otherwise," she whispered.

We stood there, impervious to time.

"I know there's much to do, but what do you say we shower together before getting serious?" I proposed.
"You beat me to it, Frank!"

We did more than scrub each other's backs, as we surrendered to the inevitable. To describe Homura's body and the immeasurable pleasure of becoming one with it belonged to a forbidden tale rooted in a special brand of esotericism. In simpler terms, I had no wish to share beyond placement: one shower stall, two people, and the act of love-making—next frame.

We didn't breach the opacity of serious matters until we finished eating the catered meal delivered at an unspecific place known only to the guards, which I immediately saw as a glaring security issue.

"It's only temporary until it gets sorted out, Frank."

"It isn't like the guards are unknown to *Adapted Control.*"

"They're obviously not, but until we can arrange for a government appointed cook, it's the best we can do. Ambrus will screen for one in the next day or two."

"Just saying—so what happened at the meeting, and why didn't we anticipate a move by *A.C.*?"

"Which question do you want answered first?"

"Let's start with the first one."

"The procedure was simple; as you already know, Eiko and I moderated by laying down the reasons for meeting without the specifics—just a serious security breach. The rest was structure, speaker order, policy, and the mundane details of keeping things flowing. Deepan and Ambrus were the speakers. When your work and identity were revealed, it was a straight shot to naming the culprit form there. But we didn't have to; Frederick Karpf identified himself with a single ominous sentence: 'The end is outside this door!' That was when *A.C.* agents entered the room to whisk him away. We realized substitutions had been made when Ambrus summoned Security. Karpf was a step ahead of the action, and we're still trying to figure out how that happened. Eiko and I are suspecting an indiscretion on the part of one member, which may warrant removal from office."

"What kind of lottery picked you guys up, if I may ask? By the look of it, it sounds like *A.C.* had its hands all over it."

"Yes, Frank, that's why you and Jillian were kept in the obscurity of the other lane."

"So you knew the selection process had been tampered with?"

"Not as much knew as suspected it had been. But only Ambrus, Deepan, Eiko, and I spoke of it. It never was a *Nine* item."

"Otherwise, I never would have made it back—I get it!"

"I don't know about that, but things would be different, for sure."

"One question that has been gnawing at me: would Jillian have been selected had she not been dead?"

"I'm inclined to think so, based on the elements of the case; and of course, I'm aware one of the primaries might just have been a hasty replacement. If you don't know that already, she died just before the selection process. So yes, you both were removed from contention by hostile manipulation."

"If you can call a murder by that name... It doesn't leave much to the imagination to get to who that replacement might be, the only one capable of an indiscretion, and with close ties to Karpf."

"Yes, Aurora and Frederick are close friends, but I have a hard time picturing her in *Adapted Control.*"

"I see her as vulnerable and easily manipulated—the perfect, unsuspecting ally."

"Something Jillian would never have fallen for, which makes a strong case for her rightful place among *The Nine*."

"It makes my heart ache, Homura, she and I were a lot closer than one can possibly imagine."

"So, you were sexual after all?"

"You're the one who said we weren't, if memory serves."

"Yes, I presumed so out of fear of the possibility. I was actually probing for the truth without admitting to it. It was an irrational response to fearing the love between us wasn't as strong as the one between the two of you. But you were wise to not heed it. Worry not; I've outgrown the discomfort."

"Glad that's out of the way! I know that from the corner of her green acre, Jillian approves of our relationship."

"I'm at peace with her wisdom."

I took a deep breath before composing my next question.

"So, what about the power of *the ambers*, and how does the activation manifest?"

"It might be compromised by Aurora's shaky position, but assuming she's alright, *The Nine* is made incommensurably stronger than the sum of its parts, which mustn't be misread as individual weakness. As components of that whole, our abilities are naturally enhanced as well. It takes the right environment for them to manifest, meaning justifiable reasons."

"And we will know that when it happens?"

"If Jillian's killer were to step in this room, you would know immediately. Do I need to spell that for you, Frank?"

"Sorry, I'm still in the process of remembering who I am."

"I understand; I'm the one who should apologize."

"So, you're saying we're a commando waiting for the right time to act; correct?"

"In a nutshell, yes."

"Weapons?"

"Yes, when applicable."

"Meaning?"

"Weapons come last, after primary skills have proven ineffective."

"I can wait to commence the class."

"You went through it already; it'll come back to you!"

A beep signaled someone was at the door. Homura let Aurora in.

Aurora: "Sorry to show up impromptu, but I don't know when else I'll muster the courage to confess to a grave error of judgment, or worse, to a moment of weakness."

Homura: "Is that about Karpf?"

Aurora: "I'm afraid to say I owe you two an apology, and Frank in particular, for having sabotaged the process to get Frederick arrested. I told him he was missed at the previous meeting, before realizing what I had said. He just smiled, so I thought I had dodged the bullet. I'm afraid I gave him the time to get prepared."

Me: "There isn't much to say to such a blatant mishap. Did you not get the meaning of him being absent at a secret meeting pertaining to his position as a traitor? I would have thought of it as rather obvious."

Aurora: "I guess it didn't register at a real level—Frederick was my friend—I felt confused."

Homura: "You do understand that such a judgmental error is unacceptable at this level. It means jeopardizing the stability of the country. It's going to be hard convincing the group you don't work for *A.C.*"

I thought Aurora was going to faint, so gaunt was her complexion and tearful were her eyes. She was only guilty of not being like the rest, a lateral thinker not entirely clued on logic. I felt bad for her.

Me: "How do you see yourself as a fighter in the group—afraid?"

Aurora: "Not at all! I just need to focus. I think I learned the lesson the hard way—I feel beyond horrible for having been manipulated by that man. It's my fault for falling for him—I just wanted to get laid."

Homura: "We don't need the florid details. Can you or not make up for it by assuming your due place among us as a fighter against the forces at the doors of government? Can you handle the responsibility without compromising the mission? I'm only asking once and I demand an immediate and convincing answer!"

Aurora: "I can."

Homura: "Then it's time to return to your quarters. This discussion never happened—get it?"

Me: "Without you, we're all compromised. I'm sure you understand what's at stake."

Aurora: "Thanks for hearing me—I know my place!"

Homura: "Thanks for having found the courage to come forward—goodnight!"

——— o ———

# 14 – THE AERIE

Ambrus flew from Vancouver. If he suspected Aurora to have spilled the beans, he didn't show it. He had secured an uncorrupted faction of Secret Services to be stationed in Squaford. In no uncertain terms, he demanded they let go of the frumpy suits for something more casual and naturally less obvious, as well as of the standard white electric sedans. "Can you look like bloody tourists for a change?!" was the underlying command. The director, John Davis, was eager to comply, since his ass was on the line for gross negligence in keeping an eye on the ins and outs of suspects across the various sectors of the agency. No news media had been contacted about the incident; *The Nine* deemed the situation too dire to support the rumors spread amongst the public by *Adapted Control*. It was already bad enough that web trolls and fringe groups were all over them in a blaze to social media frenzy. Deepan Sharma, by keeping a strong public presence, made sure the country saw nothing to it.

— o —

In the midst of all the commotion, an item emerged out of my cloudy mental process: who was Karpf, how did he manage to assume my place in *The Nine* without alerting *the ambers* or their rightful keeper, and what were the primary reasons for *Adapted Control* to wish for the dismantling of a system of government that had been so successful that the thought of existing without it was the product of madness? Of course there was the question of who were the main perpetrators behind such moral savagery. At the subsequent meeting, Ambrus Deme pointed to a few individuals capable of such willful and ill-intent "entrepreneurship."

"*Adapted Control* is the brainchild of someone with tight connections with what was once referred to as 'Deep State,' also known in some circles as the organized discontentment conglomerate of government, military, and powerful business interests. The psychological profile of the individuals involved was found to belong to the realm of criminality, and thus came the idea of a no-party government composed of representatives of the nine most important public interests. To get to the point, systems changed, but the individual thirst for control didn't just go away because of it. Deep State may be gone, but with enough bodies intent on seeing the 'old ways' revived, it is no surprise that we would, one day, find ourselves facing the such of *Adapted Control*, a rogue splinter of the old block, with a hard on for a coup d'état. I can only think of people involved with past and present governments. The ubiquity of "agent defectors" indicates the present military remains to protect borders and civilians; thus, it isn't factored in. Two names come to mind: Markus Jones from Secret Service's now defunct branch, *Acute Watch*, and Thomas Bradford, head of Security before me. Both are hardened columnists for a half-dozen extreme right-wing publications known for riling up fringe groups and elevating hostile sentiments to the status of patriotism. They are long thought to be involved in building a rogue organization. I don't doubt a link between them and *Adapted Control* should surface soon, and frankly, I'm quite surprised it hasn't yet. If anything, that may indicate that something didn't quite work as they had planned."

Lionel Watts: "What do we expect their next move to be; don't they seem to be at a disadvantage?"

Ambrus: "All we have is a warrant for Karpf's arrest, and a dead shooter. S.S. and Security are working together to uncover other rogue agents, as well as find dirt on Jones and Bradford. We have no informants in the group and no idea of their capability. We have the power, but no visibility. They have the view, and likely, enough power to inflict irreversible damage. I suggest you rethink your assessment, Lionel."

Eiko: "On a scale of one to ten, what are the odds of them finding us here before the end of the week, today being Wednesday?"

Ambrus: "On a scale of one to ten, the chance of them knowing we're presently here is five; just add one for every following day."

Suneet Kumar: "OK, let's say they have us located, what else besides watching are they going to do? With nobody inside and agents around them, I can't see how they could have the advantage. They're practically walking into a trap."

Ray Anand: "How airtight is Security after such a botched job? Can we trust our guy Davis to clean his house? What makes you say he's capable of it?"

Ambrus: "All good questions deserving of worthy answers. Unfortunately, we can only resort to speculation, and I'm afraid to say that trusting John Davis to redeem himself is a gamble on my part, which I took in the name of this group. I just hope the intuition will prove me right, if it can't prove me sane."

Aurora: "Intuition has my respect; I trust it is also honored by the rest of us."

Ambrus: "Exactly—providing it isn't confused with projection—something you may want to look into for future reference."

The slight wasn't lost to Homura and me.

Lionel: "How do we respond to an all-out attack by *A.C.*?"

Ambrus: "I understand this group has never been activated—in fact, I don't recall activation was ever required under any government—so my guess is as good as yours. Nonetheless, it's part of the acceptance package and we all have been briefed by A.I. when we got our code keys. Has anyone not heeded that chapter? I would think not, since it's the mystery item everyone goes for first. That being said, be prepared to return the fire and more!"

Aurora: "I understand weapons are the last resort."

Homura: "Right, you'll know when that time comes."

Ambrus: "Until then we'll stick to the strategy of defeating *Adapted Control* from the inside. Hopefully, our special powers will remain civil. The aim is to freeze the trigger finger. Remember, the mother of defense is composure—that's where we're at!"

Me: "What do we know about Frederick Karpf, his rank, and influences in *A.C.*?"

Deepan's holograph: "Very little, but we must reason that his accumulated knowledge of government inner workings makes him an extremely dangerous man. Since A.I. is in charge of selecting applicants, it's difficult to extract pertinent information about his person. He was last identified as the CEO of *Ground Space Labs*, a powerful multinational complex reliant on outside laws to keep itself shaded from public scrutiny. It's believed that one of its branches is financing *Adapted Control*. I'm confident I don't have to spell the significance of that datum. In other words, Karpf is a deft identity-shifter backed by massive financial resources. I strongly believe Jones and Bradford would be impotent without him, but it might be that his motives bear no resemblance to political creed."

Eiko: "Creed or not, we're dealing with the resolve to shift powers; and that means we're target number one!"

Ambrus: "Sadly, and for that reason, we'd better get prepared for an *A.C.* presence in Squaford sooner than later. Let's hope for a fair warning and a solid buffer by Security."

Deepan: "I'll keep you updated as we learn more. Until then, stay safe!"

— o —

We agreed on a couple of days of freedom before it would become necessary to stay cooped up in the *Aerie*. We arranged for pairs to go out on a shift basis for some fresh air and exercise, even though the facilities offered a training room. Nothing replaced the touch of wind and rain on the skin when the options of enjoying the outdoors suffered a setback—part of the human incongruity, I guessed. Although I would have favored Homura's company, we opted to rotate outing partner in order to keep a reliable communication flow within the group. It

93

was why Eiko and I found ourselves once again jeopardized when the first signs of trouble showed up. We were walking along the back trail to Newport Beach when we sensed more than just Secret Service following. Taking advantage of a sharp turn, we took cover and waited. Two shots broke through the nearby industrial noise before the assassin came into sight. Eiko leaped from behind with such a ferocious rear naked choke that the man fell to his knees before his face hit the ground—her body uncoiling with a violent push, so that his head was forced into the surface upon contact. I scooped his weapon and tie-wrapped his hands and feet together—part of the outing kit—before I flipped him over. Nothing could save the man with the shattered face—he was no longer breathing. The two agents were dead as well.

— o —

The feds swiftly removed the bodies before the local cops got wind of strange happenings in their town. It was paramount that secrecy prevailed for the sake of *The Nine's* safety. Of course, *Adapted Control* might have seen otherwise, but I reasoned it was too early for publicity. The event called for a regrouping.

Ambrus: "Here we have it! We all understand that *A.C.* moles are still active in Security and Secret Service, in spite of our best efforts to contain them. It means no place is safe from these guys—they'll keep on finding us wherever we go."

Eiko: "Well, Frank and I got a jump on the action; it's clear activation has given us an edge in perception and execution. I guess the shooter was meant to die because it was only my intention to neutralize him, not maim him beyond repair."

Deepan's holograph: "He died because he killed—that's the rule of balance. We can't teach these assassins new tricks—without their primary purpose, they're as good as useless—no need for concern, Eiko."

Lionel Watts: "I'm ready for action, regardless of what it takes to get rid of these assholes. I believe we've played nice long enough."

Deepan: "Activation will only permit actions in line with the protection of government and the guiding principles of civilian safety. Let's make sure to keep that line clear—crossing it isn't an option."

Homura: "I don't see a point in holing up in this building just to wait for the next surprise. We need to disperse and draw *A.C.* into traps. I don't think that the idea of defense through composure excludes forcing the opponent to move in the wrong direction."

Ambrus: "Enhanced vision is one of the assets of activation. I don't think anyone disagrees with the fact that this place poses a logistical issue—it is reinforced but not immune to a missile attack. It is becoming obvious A.I. has been compromised and that our location is no longer secret."

Me: "Based on his background, I don't doubt Karpf has a lot to do with the tweaking of A.I. What else can we dig on him? I mean, his removal pretty much guaranties the collapse of *Adapted Control*."

Deepan: "We had our chance, but we squandered it by neglecting the man's strong hold on affections, a regrettable lack of foresight and firmness on the part of the group, which sadly brings us to exposing a painful truth."

Ambrus: "The case, as we all know, was born of the inside info that a member substitution was in the realm of probability. What you may not know is that under the previous government, Frank and his partner—his twin sister, Jillian—were to return to *the lane* after completion of various assignments. I shall spare you the complex details for now, but Jillian was murdered on the *median* after a meeting with their agent, Klaus Nussbaum. The intention was to grab her body for research in what made her and Frank immune to the influence of lane-crossing. But Frank took her back to the other side before what became known as *Adapted Control* got to her, and where he stayed mourning his loss and succumbing to a decline in memory—until Nussbaum passed *the ambers* onto him. The point here is that Jillian had been pre-selected by A.I. to join *The Nine* along with Frank. Instead, Aurora ended up taking her place, in what now appears to have been the result of exterior manipulation. I'm not saying she's an *A.C.* mole; rather, she matched a specific profile that suited a close relation with Karpf. She was the unsuspecting link to gauging *The Nine's* inside temperature, so to speak."

Ray Anand: "The fact is that she's among us now, activated as we all are by the power of *the ambers*. I suggest we move on with her in the team and spend our energy addressing the real and present issue. I stand by Aurora and I hope we all do."

We all did.


The meeting came to an end. We agreed to keep two pairs in the *Aerie* and send two out, with the bodyguards, Hans and Philip, patrolling the area outside the compound in case of foul play by the feds. It had become increasingly difficult to sort out the good guys from the bad ones. As it turned out, our latest assassin was also an ex G-man.

— o —

The idea of being stuck in a converted warehouse in a small town, which by then had been uncovered by our enemies, posed a serious issue of redundancy. It was the closest to having been herded to a convenient location for *Adapted Control* to take over. They had us exactly were they wanted us, at the helm of a satellite government with metaphorical guns pointed at our heads. They knew our only viable defense was to call in the troops, but also that it was the last thing we would do, for reasons of national stability. What they had scant knowledge of, on the other hand, was the power of *the ambers*, the activation process, and the extent of that power—and so had we. Well, of course, there was Eiko's move on the assassin; something worth witnessing! I think it was safe to say that, at that very moment, she possessed something no other human in my circle had ever exhibited: insane physical speed and precision. In all certainty, she, herself, was unable to assess the scope of that fury when it happened. It was magnificent in its execution. As to me, I was practically able to see the shooter following the feds, as if spatial awareness, alerted by a glitch in the vibrational field, had sent a picture directly to my mind. One could have thought reality wasn't recognized as real when it crossed a certain threshold. If it was any indicator of things to come, I gathered we had to nurture the confidence that we weren't totally defenseless. If our

97

combined skills far exceeded the sum of our individual
ones, as we were told, I couldn't wait to see the results
with my own eyes. I guessed I wasn't the only one caught
in the thought; Homura tightened her grip around my arm
and said:

"You know what, Frank; I'm anxious to show
those guys what we're made of!"

—— o ——

# 15 – AMBER FIRE

Eiko, Lionel, Homura and I were on *Aerie* detail when we all converged on the same warning: *Adapted Control* had surrounded the town in large numbers. Under any other set of circumstances, I would have deemed it an item of intuition, but it came to us so vividly, in such a powerful single frame, that intuition was ruled out immediately. It was *the ambers* talking.

Spatial awareness kicked in like it did on the trail. I could see the bad guys like moving figures on a body heat scanner—the whole town was aglow. Ambrus's voice came on the speakers.

"We see them; they're all over! I don't think Secret Service is aware yet—so much for them being in charge of warning us!"

Eiko: "They'll know soon enough!"

Me: "Oddly, they're not on the *Aerie*; I wonder what's up with that?"

Homura: "Let's not count our blessings yet, Frank, I'm sure the feds won't miss on the opportunity to compromise us with one of their dumb moves, if we're so lucky as to still be invisible."

Lionel: "No chance of that—it's a false positive— they want us all in here; that's why they're staying clear. I suggest we vacate!"

Eiko: "I doubt they can see us like we see them. I'm with Lionel. Let's catch them from behind—I'm sure they won't expect that!"

Ambrus: "Looks like we're on a shared line; I can see you all. Are we on?"

Chorus: "Let's do it!"

— o —

By a shared line, Ambrus must have meant a common vision, as if operating from an inner room. It was the oddest of sensations, hard to describe really, but how did one translate a heightened state of consciousness into a lower one's frame? The fact was that under activation, the team became a pooled unit from which the individual drew exponentially more than it contributed. And thus, with those powers and a few weapons, team Homura and Frank split from team Eiko and Lionel without truly losing sight of each other, while still connected to the whole of *The Nine*.

— o —

The sheer number of new arrivals finally caught the attention of the local police, especially when most of the vehicles entering town were large, black SUVs. I always wondered about bad guys and black cars; one always knew trouble was abreast when they showed up in the neighborhood. Problem was *Adapted Control* convinced the cops they were after a group of mob bosses, putting our undercover Secret Service agents in the peculiar position of being hunted by both law and criminals.

It was Eiko who struck first, just as three *A.C.* agents prepared to draw fire on two feds. She was unstoppable. In one fluid move, she reduced the men to a senseless heap—it played like a movie in my head. And then, all at once, *The Nine* spread misery amid enemy forces. Surprisingly, I remained the observer, the visionary, the guide dispatching the energy of *the ambers*—the action coordinator. I saw Aurora, dodging bullets and striking mercilessly with powers drawn from the cauldrons of the underworld, unfathomable places of death and rebirth, madness and newfound sanity. Lionel pounced and crushed; Ambrus walked amid drawn fire, unscathed, as shooters broke like scorched saplings; Homura returned grown men to the womb with a barrage of crackling blue lightning that seemed to originate from the surface of her auratic shield. One by one, the glowing lights of *Adapted Control* forces faded into darkness. Soon it was all over. With the population tucked into the safety of their homes and the wised-up police out of the way, unhurt Secret Service agents started to sort through the smoldering piles to retrieve their own. By morning, Squaford had been quarantined by the military on reasons of powerful underground gas explosions responsible for toxic chemical fires; casualties among service and rescue personnel were high. As always, the residents bought into the hypnosis, and the news were quickly forgotten.

— o —

*The Aerie* was silent. Only Homura, Eiko, and I were up sipping coffee in the communal kitchen.

Eiko; "I could get used to it if I didn't know any better; talk about power! It felt like slow motion when I knew they couldn't see it come—it was awesome!"

Homura: "Blue lightning, whoa, who would have thought!? But then again, it suits me better than throwing flames."

"And me as the bearer of *amber* power, overseeing the in and out flow of our common core feeding its branches while receiving from them the energy released from the defeated!? I was mesmerized by the exponential growth of that power—it's alive in *the ambers*, and *The Nine* is made all the more potent from it!"

Eiko: "Yes, Frank, each of us in a defined role dictated by our skills—I love it! I've never felt so much alive! Did you guys see Aurora? That girl blew me away! Never mind the fuck-up with Karpf—she totally gave it to them!"

Me: "We did right in giving her the room she needed for soul-searching. She wasn't in a good place learning she was a calculated replacement for Jillian."

Homura: "Just to prove that those who thought they could manipulate A.I. were fools that ended up being played by it—a blow to Frederick Karpf, no doubt."

— o —

The rest of the team soon joined in, with more exploits recounted and a sense of family drawing us closer to what it truly meant to be *The Nine*. We knew the days left in *the Aerie* were few before a regrouping of *Adapted Control* called for an all-out battle. There were other places besides Squaford, but Karpf had the list, so we deemed Vancouver the safest place of them all.

We all left in the afternoon; Homura, Hans, and I last to depart in the armored Benz. The town and its surroundings would have been lovely to explore in another life, but I was glad to get the hell out of it in this one; a thought that was punctuated by a ground-shaking explosion. We looked around; *the Aerie* was aflame, a raging black plume rising out of the devastation amid a rain of heavy debris. A missile had hit target. We drove away ignoring the human agitation around us. We reckoned it was just another chemical explosion.

———— o ————

# 16 – PAST UPDATE

Klaus Nussbaum and Frank Marks met at the *'Sound* in Tacoma on a weekday afternoon. Frank, on top of being new in town, was also testing his footing on the opposite lane, except the *'Sound* wasn't on the opposite lane but on the *median* one, a detail he would learn about much later. In fact, Nussbaum had never been on the opposite side because nobody born on *The Lane* could travel there, except for Frank and his twin sister, Jillian.

Frank had never met Jillian; they had been separated at birth, not because their parents wanted them apart, but because the hospital had alerted the feds about a rare grouping in their DNA, which A.I. had identified as the recipe for crossing the *median lane* into opposite traffic without the side effect of going insane. *The Nine* of the time saw fit to keep dubious interests away from the news, deeming it best to destroy the paper trail and keep the twins apart. The parents were told the girl had died from respiratory failure, and Frank went on to live the life of a quiet kid with solid smarts. At age twenty-one, fresh out of college, he joined Security under Thomas Bradford, a few years before Ambrus Deme took over. Frank and Ambrus never met, but Deme knew of Frank and Jillian via a file inadvertently left behind by his predecessor, a document which he then had encrypted by A.I. and placed in a secret cache inside the vault. He took the precaution in spite of knowing the information had already been in the wrong hands, a fact that was made all the clearer when he found out Jillian had just been hired by *Ground Space Labs*, a multinational company whose North American branch was headed by Frederick Karpf.

Ambrus Deme had Jillian Meyer, née Marks, followed by Security, and then nabbed by a rescue team a few days later, under the cover of a well choreographed street shooting. She never returned to *Ground Space*, determined her future belonged among the men and women who saved her life. Within months, she had risen to the post of government agent in charge of *The Nines'* surveillance, until she too was summoned to a meeting with Nussbaum on the other side—supposedly.

By the time Frank took his first assignment, Jillian had already been working with Nussbaum for a couple of months, but the two weren't to meet until a half year later when Ambrus Deme judged the time was right for them to be reunited. The catch was they couldn't know about their biological connection until their return to *The Lane*. The reason, as illogical as it seemed, was to create an illusion of separation between them while they worked in tandem—A.I.'s notion of invisibility through the obvious: as lovers, they were less likely to be exposed as siblings.

The main reasons both were ushered by Security to the other side were twofold: for one the feds needed to know that all the trouble was worth it—there was only one way to find out—on the other hand, *Ground Space Labs* were particularly interested in figuring out a means to harvest the biology behind their unique skills for duplication and eventual marketing—something the government strongly opposed. The industry had come to a head with regulations; the technology was in place, but the catastrophic returns of those sent across had convinced inspectors to shut the program down. The only remaining option to winning approval was to apply a permanent fix to the human biological makeup, and if approval could not be won that way, a government takeover would become necessary. In the end, what Karpf and his partners truly wanted were new territories to exploit for financial gains, and what better place than one that was only minimally different, if for a mere reversal in direction. It was clear the physics had already pointed to the non-linearity of time—the human constitution solely remained the weak link. Unfortunately for Frank and Jillian, they were the ones in possession of the immediately available fix, since the hospital had destroyed their birth samples. *Ground Space Labs* with the muscle of an emerging *Adapted Control* had wagered on locating the twins, dead or alive. But Jillian had slipped between their fingers, while Bradford had failed to identify Frank Marks when he worked at Security— they concluded an insider was desperately needed.

— o —

Frank and Jillian took on liking each other on their first case. Because of their skills, they were sent to places others couldn't go, mainly to investigate what had happened to those who went and returned afflicted with irreversible psychological damage. It was also a means by which a special branch of government aptly named the *Travel Bureau* got to study how far the human mind and body could penetrate the layers of the unknown without the assistance of guiding hallucinogens and variable release tranquilizers. Jillian and Frank were active field workers, whereas practically-unconscious test specimens hooked to lab monitors were years behind providing what science and, in the case of *Ground Space*, the industry wanted now. Klaus Nussbaum, head of the *Travel Bureau*, was in charge of both overseeing cases and keeping an eye on where the scientific industrial complex might have fancied a slight overstepping of regulations into lawlessness.

— o —

Frank and Jillian had sex, meaning intercourse, only once. It happened upon returning from a particularly gruesome assignment involving a terminal reality that brought the two to the limits of their resistance to madness. It felt like the right thing to do in the name of release and the affection between them. It was good love-making, fun, but without the passions that sent lovers over the edge. They knew too much about each other for the elements of mystery to take hold—the honeymoon had happened in the womb—sex was like going out for a drink without the usual characters to provide the ambiance. They laughed about it, about Frank going limp during intercourse, about Jillian wanting to play more than she cared being sent into a sexual trance onward to the expected climax. Play was the right word for two grownups whose childhoods had been stolen.

— o —

Jillian grew up with two brothers, Clark and Justin. Clark was her senior by four years, while Justin was much older and already out of high school by the time she entered kindergarten. She liked her parents, Nancy and Lloyd, but she wouldn't say how much she loved them, because she couldn't attach love to people who poorly understood it in the first place. She thought they loved Clark by the way they catered to his very needs, but she couldn't help feel that they were just being nice to her while refraining from the elements of emotional warmth, a quality she couldn't make sense of at the level of child logic. But she loved Clark who was kind to her, unlike the bullies in the neighborhood.

While Clark went on to study business, Jillian was drawn to science at an early age. She eventually graduated with dual masters in advance physics and Assisted Migration Biology; the latter which opened the doors of *Ground Space Labs*. Although it must be said that the company's version of A.M.B. was not just reserved to plants and changing climates, but also to humans and their adaptation to new environments—the part of the science that was deemed controversial by government and religion alike.

Besides science, Jillian was drawn to martial arts, sports, and forensics—three items that pleased Klaus Nussbaum greatly by the time he became aware of her and her skills. They represented the reasons why she would one day work for the agency.

— o —

The *Travel Bureau* wasn't Nussbaum's brainchild, although nobody truly knew who had been behind it at the onset. The same was also said of Klaus, whose past was vague about his ascent in government. Needless to say the agency for which Frank and Jillian worked, *Nussbaum & Associates*, made to be believed to have existed across the *median lane*, wasn't mentioned anywhere either, and for good reasons since it didn't exist any more than the *'Sound* did in Tacoma. As already mentioned, Nussbaum only appeared to have been on the other side through the simple trickery of the center lane, including when he visited the apartment—and so did Clark when Frank and Jillian saw him on rare occasions at the house in Greenwater. Places from both sides, whether real or not, could be made into props on the *median* by a skilled manipulator—it only required minimal training to become one in the world of *The Nine*. Jillian and Frank would have known if they hadn't trusted Klaus Nussbaum, a man who was referred to them by no other than an anonymous Ambrus Deme. But the truth remained that the twins did indeed move to the other side, whence they did most of their work.

(Speaking of sides and lanes, it might be useful to clarify their positions for the sake of keeping the narrative uncluttered. Analogically, the two worlds traveled in opposite directions, while separated by a median lane, aka the neutral zone: *The Lane*—the reality of *The Nine*, and *The Other Lane*—where Frank and Jillian worked for Klaus Nussbaum out of Seattle. Of course, the "other side" applied to both lanes depending on placement. It also might be worth repeating that, because of evolutionary details, residents of *The Lane* could easily access the *median lane*, while it was inconceivable for those of *The Other Lane* to do so, since they didn't know anything about adjacent realities traveling in opposite directions on some cosmic road, unless they dreamt of it. So, in recap, Jillian and Frank, who where born on *The Lane*, were the only individuals capable of crossing the *median* onto the opposite traffic of *The Other Lane* without losing their minds. Although, as in Frank's case, it eventually came at the cost of memory—there was a limit to how much time one could spend on the other side before becoming a permanent resident and being unable to return. One may say that it took the power of *the ambers* to bring Frank back.)

— o —

The business that was keeping Clark Meyer, Jillian's step brother, in Los Angeles was no more real than any of the items that could only exist in the neutral zone. The house in Greenwater was a means to keep Frank and Jillian tethered to *The Lane*. In essence, there was a continuous interweaving between the two corridors that manifested into a seamless reality on the *median lane*. That was the nature of a successful crossing, which, in the case of the two, was experienced without the ravaging side effects others had antecedently succumbed to. Perhaps it was the way Nancy and Lloyd tiptoed around young Jillian that Clark came to suspect his little sister wasn't born into the family; regardless, the observation prompted him to avidly search for the truth. Jillian was in college when he found it amid the incoherent last words of his dying mother at the site of his parent's murder, just outside the house. It happened slightly after Ambrus came across the file upon taking charge of Security. The series of events brought the two men together in a quest for clues. It didn't take long to make the connection with the usual suspects, but the tracks went cold. Eventually, Ambrus offered Clark the job of protecting his adopted sister and her twin brother, first on *The Lane* and, later, in the neutral zone.

———— o ————

# 17 – THE ASSIGNMENT

On the day of Jillian's murder, she and Frank had met with Nussbaum at the house in Greenwater. Clark had followed them back to the threshold across from the Seattle apartment when a gunman drew fire on the twins from inside a parked black SUV. Frank suffered minor injuries but Jillian died in his arms, bleeding over the sidewalk. Frank carried her across the line onto *The Other Lane*, leaving both Clark and the killer in the blind as to their whereabouts, her body forever safe from those lusting for the mystery sealed within her. It took years before Frank was seen in the neutral zone again.

— o —

The unbearable agony of the loss took Frank Marks to the edge of the abyss. He shut the world out and steadily forgot about *The Lane*—until the dream in which Jillian came to the rescue.

"Let go, Frank, I'm happy and exactly where I want to be. Don't let your heart grow cold and your thoughts bitter because of a kink in the past. We lost and found each other once; we'll find each other again. Please, don't let the pain widen the gap between us—we exist within each other."

She was gone as she appeared, out of and back to nowhere. Frank remembered every word as if engraved in his mind, but he couldn't quite make sense of the end.

Nonetheless, that morning he got up at sunrise for a walk in the park. An overbearing weight had lifted to make room for hope and the first rays of a new happiness. He decided it was time to spend a few days at the house in Greenwater; the country air would do him good, and perhaps memories of his last day with Jillian would resonate to the tune of the recent dream. He felt relieved to experience joy instead of pain. It was true Jillian had never left him, something he had felt in the blood rushing through his veins. But now the mind had finally switched gears from reverse back to forward—he was moving towards the visible, a road of many arrows pointing to their respective horizons, some in black and white, others in saturated tones, all alive with motion from the slow to the fast. The phone rang.

"It's Klaus; you finally took it upon yourself that life was worth living after all! How you're doing, mate?"

"Surprised it took you so long to reach me; I've been at the apartment all along. I could have used the support as well as the money from the last case; what happened to you?"

"I'm not at liberty to explain; you'll understand in due time. Let's just leave it at Jillian's murder having complicated the nature of our work, as the result of which I could no longer reach you. The money and some is now in your bank account if you care checking."

"I'm not going to pretend I get any of this, but I'm willing to play the game. How are you?"

"Fine, Frank, you know, we can arrange for your return to *The Lane* if you want."

"What lane, are you sure you're alright?"

"*The Lane*, where you and Jillian came from."

"What's up with you?! If you mean our line of work, please just say so, because I'm not following the narrative here."

"Of course, Frank—just my way of saying—sorry if I confused you."

"It's alright—yes, I wouldn't mind some action."

"Great, we'll start you with small cases! Will you be at the house for a while?"

"Yeah, I'm taking a vacation from sorrow."

"I'll call you tomorrow. Don't forget to let Clark know where you are; he'll be relieved to hear from you!"

"Talk soon!"

Frank chose to ignore the fuzzy narrative. He had been out of it for too long; it was just his thoughts playing tricks. He was glad to have reconnected with both men. Of course, Clark being Jillian's brother, it wasn't hard to imagine that he endured similar trauma. Frank had chosen to shut himself out, so why expect Clark or even Klaus to reach out? He was ready to rise above the disorientation and pick up where he had left off, but much had happened to him since the last assignment, most notably, a complete memory wipeout about his true origins and *The Lane*. He had moved his past to *The Other Lane* instead, and now there was only one world left. The only viable link was Clark's house, the one path left for Frank to reach the neutral zone, whereas before Jillian's murder, it only took the wish to connect to be there. The inconvenience was the most felt on Nussbaum and Ambrus Deme, who were in the midst of defining *Adapted Control* and the dilemma of A.I. having chosen Frederick Karpf as one of the nine members of government. The ex-Security director, who was also selected to join the governing body, had established a connection between Jillian's assassination and Frank's absence from *The Lane*, as being part of the irregularities perceived at his end. It didn't take him long to build a case, in which Nussbaum's imperative role was to put Frank on it.

Ambrus gathered Deepan Sharma and Homura Oshiro to discuss the ways to bring Frank back to his old self and due place. It was Deepan who thought of *the ambers*.

— o —

The amber set which had been *cleansed* in a ritual performed by a spiritual appointee—a practice applied with every change of government—was kept in the possession of the high governor of *Synthesis*, the crossbreed assembly of religious leaders and top scientists, past, present, and future. Ambrus Deme knew what he was up against when he requested permission to borrow the nine amber tetrahedrons, but his high clearance eventually convinced *Synthesis* it was for the highest of causes.

— o —

It took nearly a year between the Jillian dream and the perfect time to hand over the amber set to Frank. Meanwhile, elaborate paths had been established for connections other than in the Greenwater house. And so, on one sunny Saturday morning, Klaus Nussbaum brought the set out and sent Frank on his new assignment with nary a list of instructions, except for, "Each contains

115

an identical set of three items that have been shuffled for safety. In other words, they'll need matching again. Take them; you'll know what to do with them when the time comes—good luck!"

———— o ————

# 18 – KLAUS NUSSBAUM

Homura and I snuggled in the back of the Mercedes—we were mentally drained from battle. It totally felt like we had been set up from the moment of Karpf's choreographed escape from the government building. *Adapted Control* agents had been after me on three occasions with the intention of either killing me or arresting me—actually four, with the inclusion of Jillian's murder in Seattle where I was also a target. It was my DNA they were after—government was just in the way. The paradox was that by rescuing me from oblivion, the group, as it stood, had put me in harm's way in order to save the integrity of the governing body of which I was part and Jillian meant to be. The way I saw it, Karpf was a bigger motherfucker than recently thought. He was one of the heads of *Ground Space Labs*, and I wouldn't have been surprised if the report had shown him having overseen the failures of cross-lane travel.

Homura turned her head to look me in the eyes.

"What are you thinking, Frank; you seem so far?"
"Making sense of what sent me to the other side in relation to what brought me back. It all seems connected somehow. Jillian was killed by *Ground Space* hitmen, wasn't she?"
"It appears so, Frank, but we couldn't know that until Karpf was exposed as an impostor. We had to put our trust in A.I. for the selection. Now we're facing a break in logic that might send us back to the enactment of

the no-party government, now vulnerable to the whims of corrupt intelligent machines."

"Unless there's no corruption, and A.I. had to pick the best case scenario. Remember, we make the computers—they don't make us."

"So you're saying it's possible Karpf was chosen on purpose, even though it appears he wiggled his way in by corrupting the system?"

"Just an intuition. What better way to make a thief comfortable than to give him the keys to the house, if you get my drift? In the meantime, A.I. can work in the background—unimpeded."

"And what indicates A.I. is doing so—I don't see how it's helping us win this conflict?"

"We're activated, that's how."

"What does A.I. have to do with *the ambers*?"

"Perhaps how they ended up in my hands?"

"I'm sure Ambrus can clarify; he's the one who solicited a favor from the high governor."

"And the man just handed the set over to Ambrus so that he could give it to Klaus Nussbaum for me—a then permanent resident of the other side, and blindfolded to boot—to figure out how to put them back together, while working on what appeared to be a backwards assignment at the time? No extra persuasion, it just sufficed to ask, right?"

"Don't be sarcastic, baby, I'm just suggesting— but I see the validity of your point."

"The crux of the matter, as I see it, is that if we don't start eliminating the superfluous in favor of the fundamental, we're soon going to be swinging at empty space. We have to start thinking of *Adapted Control* as just a brunt, witless, rogue element *Ground Space* uses as its expandable ramrod. When the dust settles, all Karpf'll have to do is pick and choose from amid the rubble. I say we hit *Ground Space* where it hurts: by reducing their bankable assets to ashes."

"Are you talking reputation, financial history, status, property, what are you aiming at, Frank? The company exists behind a shield, impervious to outside pressures."

"Not impervious to those it owes money or favors to—be they banks or donors with deep pockets—if suddenly their financial structure were to expose a fissured foundation."

"And how do you propose to do that?"

"By finding the crack."

— o —

It might have sounded like an unsteady concept; thus, I couldn't blame Homura for her skepticism, but it came from somewhere reminiscent of a theme of common corruption. Those desperate for gains, either already had established fortunes or were about to lose them. There was a fifty percent chance that the branch of *Ground Space Labs (G.S.L. America)* headed by Karpf, and suspected of financing *Adapted Control*, belonged to the category walking on thin ice. After all, as I recently learned, they were the ones whose research on lane travel was shut down by regulators after a series of badly publicized experiments. I figured it amounted to a major setback, and perhaps, just perhaps, some investors had gotten antsy. I didn't imply *Adapted Control* was no longer a threat; I simply suggested that by pulling the tit from the mouth, we had a chance of weakening the beast.

It was obvious that my idea lacked a proper convincing argument, but I couldn't help seeing it as a viable offensive move with clear ramifications. *The Nine's* error was in undervaluing Karpf to a mere insider when he was in fact the brain of the operation, and the one responsible for the attacks, including Jillian and her adoptive parents' killings. The thought carried a blessed feeling about my own parents' ignorance of the separation and the hospital lie—likely the reason why they were still alive.

The whole thing transposed me back to the resort and the murder of the two feds. Of course, Karpf saw to it since they were there to protect me and not just *The Nine*. It was becoming clear I already was a target then, and that Homura was possibly shielding me from being killed. So, who was the assassin, Jeremy the bartender? Very unlikely, even in a world full of smoke and mirrors. No, I was starting to believe Karpf did his share of the dirty work, and most plausibly took care of the feds on one of his hikes. That was it; Lazarus and Gomez accompanied him, knowing he couldn't do anyone any harm! It was obvious Ambrus and Homura had long suspected him to be the bad guy, but without confirmation from *the ambers* and the following activation, there was nothing much they could do. Although his assisted escape from the administrative building sealed his culpability as a criminal, it did little to put him at odds with the law, since *Adapted Control's* main aim was to turn justice on its head with a government takeover.

We were approaching North Vancouver. Homura straightened up to look out the tinted glass. On some level, it was a blessing that *A.C.'s* first offensive had happened away from the big city and the scrutiny of the press, but I saw no objection to publicity in regard to reporting *Ground Space's* financial standings. I was ready to see to it!

— o —

Upon arrival, I pressed Ambrus to put me in touch with Klaus Nussbaum.

"Glad you finally asked; I was just wondering when that connection might happen. What stopped you from just calling his number?"

"We had an arrangement: no calls until the end of the assignment. I figured he might reconsider if it came from you."

"Don't you think your assignment is over by now? Finding your way back to *The Lane* was it—you were done when you put *the ambers* in their proper order and found your rightful place among us."

"Well, you could say that I needed to put my thoughts in their proper order as well. Why don't you call him; he'll get a kick out of it, I'm sure."

Klaus Nussbaum called back within the hour.

"Congratulations, Frank, I'll be in Vancouver tomorrow—driving from Seattle—I'll give you a ring when I get there!"

Of course, he meant the Seattle of *The Lane*— there wasn't a need for the neutral zone anymore, at least between us. I would eventually cross *the median* to visit

121

Jillian's grave, but there were other fish to fry for the moment.

— o —

Homura and I deemed the penthouse to be as safe as any other place in Vancouver. As long as *The Nine* remained scattered, there was a greater chance *Adapted Control* couldn't deploy simultaneous attacks on all of us—they needed us in a tight spot like in *the Aerie* or any of the government structures. They could still incrementally destroy us, but the risk would increase with every assault, at which point the option of keeping the media machine from noticing and sending public opinions reeling in the wrong direction would become unrealistic. They were playing their game on the fine balance of strategy and history was filled with too many fools for them to not heed the consequences of a bad move. That being said, the top of a tower was an easy missile target, but again, I didn't see how they could find my DNA amid the rubble, which brought me to thinking that the destruction of *the Aerie* was mostly for show. At that point, I came to realize that *Adapted Control* might have been a tad too low-browed for *Ground Space*'s traditional reliance on the discretion of lone shooters. As if she had read my mind, Homura, coming out of the shower naked, wet, and dangerously sensual, offered:

"*Ground Space* has lost control of *A.C.*—Jones and Bradford are fanatics who strongly believe they're about to win some kind of war against an imagined threat they see in a government catering to ultimate democracy. They don't feel at home without feuding political parties, propaganda, adversity, or whatever feeds their developmentally arrested, paranoid and intolerant little brains. They're cretins basking in the support of other cretins; that's about all there is to it. Karpf was a fool to think he could use them as his foot soldiers—they just want to see the world burn."

"And that came to you when you were showering?"

"It came to me when the massage jets hit the right spot. When was the last time we fucked, Frank?"

— o —

Hans and Philip let Nussbaum in right after dinner. Homura had just left for a meeting with Ambrus. I asked of her to mention my idea of hitting *Ground Space America* with a damaging financial report. She said she would, but to not expect much until I came up with a solid plan. Well, that was why I wanted Klaus in—I came to the point right after catching up with the times.

"What kind of dirt can you dig on *Ground Space Labs*? I have the strange feeling Karpf's sector is financially vulnerable as the result of funneling shitloads of money into *Adapted Control*. I'm thinking freefalling stock prices and closing the tap on *A.C.*"

"Well, I was thinking it'd have been a good assignment for you, but since you don't work for me anymore, I might as well work for you. I spent the entire last year studying them and gathering as much data as I could on how they run their operation. It's a mastodon crossbred with an octopus, but there isn't much left resisting me. Which tentacle should be cut first?"

"Since I'm not trying to bypass *The Nine*, let's just explore the possibilities. Did Karpf have to borrow money to finance *A.C.*, and against what bankable assets?"

"He did from two sources: the parent company, *Ground Space International*, moneys insidiously diverted from the lane travel program, and *Borga Bank*, the multi-headed financial behemoth known to resort to special methods to find money when there's none left, if you get the drift. It all depends on where and how you plan on inflicting the damage."

"Too much too fast is out of question. I want finesse, subtlety. How do we scare Karpf enough so that he cuts supplies to *A.C.*? Those guys need to be brought down first. Is their fleet of SUVs paid for, if not, how do we get the manufacturer to switch the drive off on each of the vehicles? Same with their missiles; can we disable them remotely? Then when they're on their knees, we hit Karpf and *Ground Space*."

"I don't remember you being such the fast thinker and talker—is Homura doing this to you?"

"*The Other Lane* slowed me down, methinks. No, Homura grounds me, on top of completing me. We found each other the same way Jillian and I found each other, via duplicity on your part, if memory serves."

"Glad you didn't lose your sense of humor. I wish Jillian was still with us though."

"She told me we lived in each other—I believed her. She's never too far, Klaus."

"I believe that too, Frank."

He promised to get back to me about the plan. He would be in Vancouver for another week before returning to Seattle. I wondered what was in Seattle that demanded his presence, it couldn't just be *Nussbaum & Associates*—Jillian and I were the associates. One never knew with Klaus.

— o —

It had been three days since the Squaford attack, and still no news from the Jones/Bradford boys. I very much doubted that the destruction of *the Aerie* hadn't contained the message of a promise of retaliation. Security had been instructed to hold off the customary protection so that we could immediately neutralize whoever pretended to be covering our backs. A few body bags went the usual places under the watch of Eiko—Hans took care of the routes. We couldn't stop the stealthy primary; she had found her place amid the lanes and was determined to purge the place of its shifters and crawlers. But those weren't *Adapted Control*; they answered directly to Karpf. They were the Security renegades, exes and wannabes, provided by yet more influential traitors tucked in the layers of government. Ambrus Deme and Deepan Sharma had put together an investigating team to see to the combing of Secret Service and the entire Security sector, hoping the infestation hadn't spread too far into critical areas.

*The Nine* regrouped for a short meeting at one of the secret rooms provided for emergency sessions. We were all prepared for a power display by *A.C.*, but we also were concerned about the dangers such an attack posed on civilians. It was a good time to bring my idea of working from the inside out. The single objection came from Ray Anand, who doubted time was on our side for such an intricate process. But Aurora came to the rescue.

"We could just do nothing and wait, or wait for our work to bear its fruit. So far, we've done nothing but counterattack. We've let the suches of Karpf and his cronies walk all over the system, kill our people, corrupt government, and yet all we think about is when the next attack is due?! We pride ourselves in our defense, which if I must remind you all, only exists because Frank here, after managing to survive life on *The Other Lane*, put order to our affairs, but when the going gets tough, we show a cold shoulder when Frank introduces the notion of an offense?! Do you want to be remembered as the soft government that brought fascism back to the masses, or as the one that brought meaning to evolution? For the sake of using a football analogy, let's recognize that there are two sides to the field. Frank is bringing an offensive move to the game—I say we play!"

Rarely was an oral item followed by silence, but Aurora managed to leave the group mesmerized; particularly me, who couldn't help but hear Jillian in her words. What was happening to my poor head? Needless to say, she catalyzed sentiments towards a conclusive acceptance of my plan—Nussbaum and I were on, and Aurora had showed once and for all where she belonged!

— o —

I met with Klaus at a coffee shop not far from where Eiko and I had been chased by bullets. It was a risk which I knew could put me in harm's way, but I was tired of being cooped up in Homura's place. I was a street level kind of guy who fancied sidewalks full of people and the leaves falling on patio furniture while sipping mochas. I also knew Hans and Philip couldn't be too far; Homura made sure of it.

"I have some stuff ready for shipping, if you don't mind hearing about it." Klaus said.

"I'm all ears, mate!"

"The beauty with A.I., Frank, is that if you know your way around, you can make friends in the oddest of places. A memo containing, let's say, 'pertinent data,' and inconspicuously sent to the right investors, can go a long way. I just happen to have such a friend deeply embedded in the world of finance, *who* was quick to pinpoint the irregularities *it* found in the *G.S.L.* compounded info sent its way. All *it* had to do was reference it with *International Live Database*, a place not accessible to humans."

"And you did that how, exactly?"

"I've been around long enough to go places, Frank, that's all you need to know for the moment. So what do you think about sending some *G.S.L. America* stocks down the slope?"

"Just enough to scare Karpf, but nothing that would make him look our way, right?"

"Rest assured, just a wee memo, Frank."

"And what about shutting the fleet and the missiles down?"

"Consider their SUVs and two choppers done; as to the missiles, without the choppers, they're useless. We could also arrange to have them detonate at your convenience if you want to keep the birds in the air. You strategize, I deliver; if the arrangement is to *The Nine's* satisfaction, it works for me!"

"I have the go ahead; we're on with the stock market! Then, we can tackle the rest when supplies to *A.C.* stop flowing."

"I knew you'd go that route; it practically feels like the good old days!"

The thought couldn't have been further from occurring to me.

—— o ——

# 19 – AURORA

*Ground Space Labs America* stocks tumbled on a day of heavy trading, barely a few hours after memos hit the desks of select investors. A.I. didn't consider info based on criminal activity to be insider trading. It was just plain logic that irregularities should be followed by their own chains of events. No law was broken if some nudging by a small article in a business paper should so happen, even if in the form of an innuendo—rumors were allowed. It also happened that accounts tied to *A.C.* were garnished by lenders, notably *Borga Bank* which always kept an eye on their investments' health reports. The diversion of borrowed monies to radical organizations they didn't control was enough for the financial giant to put their lawyers to work. It didn't even have to be their money; they defined "proximity" as their turf.

I suspected the phones were ringing on Frederick Karpf's desk, but he wasn't around. Instead he had been spotted by S.S. driving south towards the industrial zone of Annacis Island where *Adapted Control's* new fleet of SUVs was awaiting his signature for release. Klaus explained that Bradford, who was in charge of picking the rides up with one of his crews, had been turned down for lack of funds in the organization's accounts.

I never thought of Nussbaum as being a big fish. After all, we were associates; he shopped for cases, while Jillian and I took care of field work. But it turned out his reach was significant, by far eclipsing that of the old team. His access to A.I. was already scary, but he was now tracking Karpf on his laptop, as a stream of information about the man, *Ground Space*, and *A.C.* was being delivered in real time. Homura and Eiko sat with us around the low concrete table of the tearoom, following the news. The rest of *The Nine* was also wired to the system, watching from their respective safe spaces.

At the end of Belgrave Way, Karpf made a left and then a right into the massive car lots where thousands of new vehicles were parked before finding their ways into dealerships. He pulled next to the *Adapted Control* crew bus where he was soon seen approaching Bradford on foot. Some sort of exchange took place before a third body joined in. In the meantime the stream flashed: "Thomas Bradford denied for lack of funds," and then came the coup de grace: "Frederick Karpf not authorized to transfer funds to *Adapted Control's* accounts." I could have sworn I saw Bradford take a swing at Karpf, but it could have just been wishful thinking. The two vehicles left the lot—Karpf racing ahead at unsafe speeds.

"That's all for now, folks!" Klaus said.

Eiko: "I'm impressed; it looks like you and Frank put some serious work into it. I only have one request though: don't get too greedy—I still want in on the action!"

Klaus: "I'd say *The Nine* isn't quite done yet judging by the fact you're still activated. Give them a few days to find their bearings around the anger and you'll have your work cut out, Ms. Kohno."

Homura: "I'm so glad Aurora came forward; it was a game-changer—such depths!"

"You may say that; I mistook her for Jillian for a second."

"*The ambers* know, Frank!"

— o —

I was dying to connect with Aurora, so I left a message with her to join me for coffee at one of the West End places. It was a shot in the dark, but I felt pretty relaxed about the possibility of her showing up. This time, I didn't tell anyone where I was going, not even Hans. I snuck out like a thief and went out the one-way, self-locking service doors in the back of the building. No-one noticed my escape. I wasn't running away from Homura, far from it, but I craved a moment to myself—danger included—so that I could feel the beat of my heart and the blood running through my veins. This was personal; Homura would understand—she always did.

Aurora didn't show up, or rather, it was what I thought. Then the place filled up with big guys with an attitude; I could tell they were armed and extremely dangerous. The reason I knew was because my senses suddenly reached maximum receptivity. My mind was crunching impossible calculations around my best options at getting out unscathed, but it didn't want to settle on a conclusive scenario. I saw a series of moves that would get me half way there, but it got fuzzy after that; it looked like death waiting by the door—my own. I lunged at the two closest bodies and sent them crashing into chairs and tables. A gun was drawn and fire came my way, but the bullet was slow-moving and missed me. Two more bodies came down, irreversibly broken—more fire—I was no longer seeing, hearing, or feeling; my body was flowing in between flying objects, thrust fists and feet—it knew the moves, anticipated action with remarkable precision, but I was getting closer to the point where my mind couldn't make out the rest. And then, out of nowhere, an opening allowed me to squeeze into it, just in time to dodge a flurry of bullets. I saw Aurora turning flesh to ashes amid melted plastic and white-hot metal, the place was burning as we hit the street. We were gone before witnesses could make sense of it.

We sat by the water of Lost Lagoon, Aurora leaning against me—it felt right.

"I knew not to come in too early—I waited outside. I couldn't imagine you being by yourself without trouble lurking; I'm sorry."

"I was ready to take a chance to meet with you. Something's been nagging at me since the meeting and I needed us to be alone. Maybe I should have chosen this place instead of the café."

"Same difference, they were after you the minute you left the tower."

"And how would you know that?"

"Because I was following them before I took the lead to wait across the place. If I were you, I wouldn't trust my phone anymore."

"You saved my life, Aurora."

"Well, you put a hell of a fight, pretty impressive, really. So, what brings us here, Frank?"

"This might sound weird, but have we met before, I mean, before *The Nine*? The way you spoke reminded me of a voice I once heard years ago."

"I'm sure we didn't, because I don't see how we could have met without me having a crush on you. You would have known!"

"Since we're between grownups, do you have a crush on me now?"

"You're safe, Frank, Karpf cured me of that affliction; plus Homura and I are sisters."

"You mean sisters as in girlfriends, right?"

"No, Frank, sisters as in twins."

OK, I couldn't say the news didn't take me by surprise. Actually as was floored, as in weakened by impact. It was a one-hit knocker that sent me reeling like a drunken puppet. I intuited Aurora expected me to have a powerful reaction by the way she squeezed her body against mine as in implicating that she and I were as good as brothers and sisters, which in the context of comparing her to Jillian made some sort of crazy sense.

"Why didn't Homura make mention of it?"

"Because she doesn't know yet. We were separated at birth for the same reasons you and Jillian were—DNA."

Two hits in a row—I was ready to beg for mercy.

"And when do you plan on telling her?"

"That's when you come in, Frank; I count on you for that. Let's say, as a favor for having saved your life?"

"Only if you can convince me of the reason why you would know when she doesn't!"

"Perhaps you should ask yourself why her parents sent her away when you two were children."

"That's not enough!"

"I know; I wasn't finished. Jillian's brother, Clark, can tell you—my adoptive parent's were murdered one day after Jillian's were. I know of the killings because Ambrus rescued the both of us—that's how we met."

"You knew Jillian?!"

"We became friends before she was sent to *The Other Lane*."

"You're kidding me!? Do you know where Homura's parent sent her; I was told it was because of me?"

"It wasn't; she went where you too ended up going. It's complicated, but both your parents stayed with you in the neutral zone when you and Homura actually lived on *The Other Lane*, except apart from each other. The three lanes were meant to look like one."

"Tell me you don't know the mastermind behind all of it!"

"I'll let you figure that one out!"

"What happened to you after the murders?"

"The same that happened to Jillian and you—save for the location—I was in L.A. As to why I ended up replacing Jillian in *The Nine* and holding Frederick Karpf's dick, there is more to that story than meets the eye. Let's just say that I know a thing or two about assignments. Convinced?"

"That will do. But I count on you to tell me one day why you warned Karpf of his upcoming arrest."

— o —

Aurora and I parted at the bottom of the tower. We had stayed by the water a long time saying nothing, our bodies close to one another, like old friends who no longer had anything to hide and fear from each other. It was definitely sensual and I didn't doubt sex would have been a given under different circumstances. Love was a funny thing, with so many hands in so many pots. That night, it felt like it had allowed us to touch the sky.

— o —

It was very late, Homura was up—I could sense deep anxiety the second she spoke.

"I missed you, Frank! For a while I thought you were gone, like forever. What happened, and why didn't you tell me you were going out?"

"I'm sorry, I needed the space. Things came up that needed clarifying with Aurora, but there was also trouble when *A.C.* sent a dozen bruisers to kill me."

"I knew it! I guess you pulled out of it intact."

"Not without Aurora's help—we neutralized them all and left the place ablaze."

"So, that was you and not another blown underground gas line!?"

"I don't think they can keep this one away from the press; there were witnesses."

"So were there in Squaford—and not a peep!"

"We'll see how that pans out. In the meantime, we need to talk. Are you alert enough to skip a night's sleep?"

Homura and I held each other for a long time before hitting the kitchen for tea. It was so poignantly touching to see this powerful woman becoming so fragile around love and loss. I wouldn't have been surprised if her present emotions were tied to a confusing past; I sure found mine brought to the open by Aurora's revelation.

I told Homura everything that was said by the water, as well as my physical closeness to her sister. She took it without showing surprise or disbelief; rather, she seemed relieved, like a weight had been lifted.

"I find it extraordinary that our lives should be so intertwined with parallels. Now I get why things didn't always add up after I was sent away. And you too, even though they made it look like you never left. How does it feel to realize that your life on *The Other Lane* started at such an earlier time?"

"From the perspective of an older self I feel robbed of the truth, but I don't think I would have understood the truth then. I assume it was the only option to keep us safe from those who wanted to know what made us. Something must have happened that jeopardized the secrecy of our makeup—someone got wind of it even though all traces had been erased."

"Well, for one thing two sets of parents knew one of their twins had died at birth, I bet from similar conditions. Maybe the same individual heard both stories and got curious. Of course, it would have to have been someone looking for something specific. Too far-fetched?"

"Nothing's too far-fetched in this business; all we need is the sketch, not the details. If you remember, Ambrus came across a dossier about Jillian and I; what stops us to envision that a similar file about you and Aurora also existed? And guess whose hands it might have fallen into? One thing leads to another, my love, and I wouldn't be surprised if the murders of Aurora and Jillian's adoptive parents were tied to Jillian's killing in Seattle and all the attempts on my life here."

"Heavy, but that doesn't explain why no attempts were made on me and Aurora."

"You forgot the shooting on the waterfront. If I hadn't brought you down just as the shots were fired, you may not be here now. As to Aurora, I wonder if they didn't mix her with Eiko, she's the one who was targeted on at least two occasions. But I wager Aurora is stealthier than we think and she's been ahead of those guys all along. She's definitely not what we all perceived her to be; I believe she's been after Karpf from the get-go."

"That'd be my sister! I can't believe it, Frank, why didn't she want to tell me herself?"

"Because she knew the story would be more convincing if it came from me—that simple!"

———— o ————

# 20 – THE LAST BATTLE

Based on Ambrus's latest report, the investigating teams at National Security and Secret Service had rounded up enough bad seeds to put a freeze on those who might have thought defection was an investment in job futures. *Adapted Control* was all alone. And so was Frederick Karpf who, according to Klaus's inside news, had been fired as CEO of *Ground Space Labs America*. Additionally, multiple warrants had been issued for his arrest in a powerful flexing of existing laws. Order was slowly being restored in government.

On the day following the attack on my person, Klaus sent the signal to shut the fleet down, just in time to prevent an all-out orchestrated mission on *The Nine*. All SUVs stalled at once, and not necessarily in ideal places. Police intervened, shots were heard. One of the choppers aiming for the tower exploded over the Harbour in a big orange ball, shrapnel narrowly missing some of those who came to enjoy some peace on the waterfront—irony never slept. The second bird stalled upon take-off and came down crashing on the roof pad, killing pilot and passengers. But there were more coming out in droves, armed fanatics in kakis, brandishing Kalashnikovs, bazookas, and even bayonets. The public dissipated in routs, as *The Nine* prepared for action. As expected, Eiko struck first, taking on the dumbest of the brawn. I swore I heard her shout, "Bring on the beef!" There wasn't a doubt she favored the biggest motherfuckers of the lot; she had a chip on her shoulder the size of a log, and she was about to get rid of it by ramming it up some sorry ass. It was the best way to describe where she was at, bad words for bad pain. That girl had a story she didn't want to tell, but it was obvious it included big white men with the most sordid of intentions. I could see all of the team in my field of perception: Eiko, Deepan, Ray, Aurora, Ambrus, Lionel, Suneet... Homura was nearby watching my back, me watching hers. There were no pictures of incomplete paths anywhere, like there had been at the café where I saw my life momentarily put on standby. The power of *the ambers* had the situation under control. All crumbled when Homura frantically called my name.

"Frank, check Aurora, I think she's in trouble!"

How had I been unable to see it?! Karpf had joined the fight, sneaking from behind. I heard the shot explode in my mind's ear. I didn't know how I made it clear across town, but my body was there right between Aurora and the bullet, just in time for me to push her aside. I got hit on the shoulder—a graze wound—I sprang up to face the man who had killed Jillian. There was no time for unnecessary drama, no stretching of the action into a long, single tension. I struck Karpf to the side of the head with such ferocious velocity that his neck ripped open in a bloody mess of muscles and arteries. It wasn't punishment I was after; I simply strived to get rid of the vermin. Aurora finished the job before wrapping her body around mine.

"Now that you saved my life, I think I have a crush on you, hero!"
"I hope you're not serious—here comes Homura!"

Homura: "Am I calling at a bad time?"
Aurora: "Just this one time, sister, I promise!"

I was glad Homura wasn't the jealous kind, because for *that* one time, I wanted to feel her sister all over me, inside me, until she and Jillian became one. I sensed it was also Jillian's wish, the Jillian that forever lived in my blood.

— o —

*Adapted Control* was defeated. Ambrus had taken down both Jones and Bradford. He could have dragged them into custody but he didn't see a point of wasting judicial resources. The lesser the public knew about what he considered the private matters of *The Nine*, the better for conspiracies to not be given a chance to ferment. There would be plenty of news about what happened— about the mafia, street gangs, the usual suspects, all playing a role in a drama that could only exist somewhere out there, while government made sure everybody was safe.

— o —

We were deactivated. The amber set was returned to *Synthesis* in the order I had put it—its just order until the next call for action.

Homura and I took off for California—our private honeymoon. I also had my reasons to want to meet with Clark Meyer in Los Angeles where I believed a link to my personal chain could be found. All the more personal since I had allowed Aurora's energy to mix with my own. Clark had answers to my questions, the first one being why he chose to make himself hard to get by holing up in Southern California, with Aurora suspiciously across from him on *The Other Lane*. I needed to know his role in the concealment of his adopted sister, his connection to Klaus if any, and where he fitted in the present picture.

Because of my closeness to Jillian and Aurora, I could have given the impression that I wasn't serious about my relationship with Homura. To set the record straight, I had a crush on her as a child and I was madly in love with her as we drove down the Pacific Coast. We couldn't get enough of each other's bodies and minds. We stopped so frequently for sex that we gave up on planning ahead. We adopted the philosophy that our destination was the trip—not the arrival. I couldn't recount the many ways we played with each other, laughing, moaning, climaxing, laughing again. It was our honeymoon alright, and we were fearless about squeezing every drop out of it—figuratively, metaphorically, whatever. We were still riding on the high of *the ambers* and we hoped it'd last forever. Of course, the sex was only the surface of our love for each other—I admired her as much as she did me, and for that we counted our blessings. Even though I disliked the *soul mates* label, it was what we were.

——— o ———

# 21 – CLARK MEYER

I met Clark at his office. He let me know he was glad to see me, but he couldn't stop asking why I had driven all the way down from British Columbia to Los Angeles to meet with him. He didn't seem to buy the bit about the honeymoon, although he should have. Perhaps it was his way of saying he was sorry for disappearing after Jillian's death, or maybe he didn't approve of my relationship with Homura. At any rate, I found his behavior odd. I went straight to the point.

"So, the house in Greenwater, the business in L.A.; all in the neutral zone, right?"

"Well, I'm sure you caught up with the deceit by now, but I wouldn't call it that when it was meant to save your life, as well as Jillian's. I'll be honest with you, Frank, my job was to keep an eye on you both, to protect you, but when it mattered most, I failed you. You were brave enough to take her across the line, so that motherfucking Fred Karpf wouldn't violate her dead body. I'll never forgive myself for it!"

"Please, explain how you ended up watching our backs."

"After my parents were murdered and Jillian was moved out of harm's way by Security on Ambrus Deme's orders, I ended up connecting with the man and eventually working for him. That was when he put me on the job."

"Were you aware that Jillian and I had never met him, even though she worked for him on government detail, as I did after he took over from Bradford? What were his reasons for staying in the shadow?"

"I think it's clear he knew he was being watched by Karpf who was fresh out of *Acute Watch*."

"Any logic behind me being kept in the dark about this? I was aware of Markus Jones's role in *Acute Watch*, but Karpf!? Who else knows about it?"

"Besides me and Ambrus, not the vaguest idea. I've no clue as to why he never mentioned it to you. Maybe you two never had a chance to get there."

"Possibly, but it's now water under the bridge—both Jones and Karpf are dead. I'm sure you heard."

"I have my sources."

"What's your angle on others like Jillian and I?"

"There could be many, but I only know of a second set of twins."

"Does Homura Oshiro ring a bell?"

"Never heard of her."

"What about Aurora?"

"I was afraid you'd ask. I don't think many people know her real name, and for good reasons. But because, and only because Karpf, Jones, and Bradford are gone, I feel the time is right to tell you. Her name's Ena Karpf, Frederick's adopted sister."

Anything new about Aurora felt like a punch!

"What does her birth certificate say?"

"That part of her past is missing."

"This is too much! Who the fuck killed Karpf's parents then, if not him or his friends?"

"He killed mine; that's for sure, but I doubt he did his old folks in."

"You understand what that means don't you? Do we need yet another villain? For God's sake, Clark, be straight with me; I have no time for bullshit!"

"I might fuck up, but I never lie; I always thought it was somebody with a grudge."

"And you're sure you know nothing about Aurora's twin sister?"

"I swear, the trail went cold when I looked for her."

"OK, what about Klaus Nussbaum then; what's your connection with him?"

"Besides the *Associates*, he ran the *Travel Bureau*, an odd outfit tied to government since the onset of the no-party system, that's how we connected. We designed cases for travelers to test their physical and mental limits."

"You did what?!"

"Yes, *Nussbaum & Associates* was a front for the *Travel Bureau*; you and Jillian were the test subjects, and so was Ena under my watch."

"Motherfuckers! I can' believe this shit!"

"To our credit, we also kept the bad guys from putting their dirty hands all over you, so give us a break, will you, Frank!?"

"Alright, I buy that, any other nasty surprises?"

"We're done bro; so who's the new girl?"

"You don't deserve to know, but what the hell— she's Aurora's twin sister, Homura Oshiro, the one you never heard about."

It was Clark's turn to take a direct hit and I was glad for it! I couldn't wait to return to the hotel and tell Homura about the latest. I was sure questions would fly the minute she'd hear about her sister and Frederick Karpf's relationship. But I wasn't quite finished with Clark Meyer.

"One favor, mate; Homura and I are planning on hopping over to *The Other Lane*. So, for good time's sake, we're going to need Ena's old address, and from there we'll connect with you in the neutral zone. Is that something that resonates with you?"

"Son of a bitch, Frank, have you lost your mind?!"

"Not at all, Homura and I would fancy a bit of the old country, so what better place than across a trusted friend's pad?"

"Well, it's your honeymoon after all, consider it a wedding present!"

"The wedding hasn't been planned yet, but thanks all the same. I'll introduce you to the future bride in the neutral zone. Cheerio!"

— o —

All of a sudden, I felt drained. The idea of telling Homura about the machinations of men with too much time on their hands made me noxious. The whole thing had the taste of a bad dream on a hangover morning. In spite of their best intentions, we served their power game, their need to manipulate for the satisfaction of primal urges. What they called the right thing to do, or, the only option, was nothing short of a play of words, simple logical fallacies that blinded in their very simplicity. Of course, it was a lie, and Jillian's death was the proof of it. They got careless, arrogant; they could not even build a defense—they had me, Jillian, Aurora, Homura and the rest of the gang do the dirty work instead. They designed cases; that was what they did, and then showed up for the grand finale to claim the glory. I so hoped I was totally wrong about it!

— o —

It was the first time since the beginning of the trip that I didn't desire Homura's naked body. Clark's words and energy were sticking to me like a parasitic skin over my own, a coat that clogged its pores—asphyxiated. A shower sounded like good medicine, and since Homura insisted on joining me to sponge away the nature of my discomfort, I deemed resisting to be futile—we had sex after all and a wrong was promptly righted. We lay on our backs, side by side.

"Frederick Karpf was Aurora's adoptive brother. Any idea why she wouldn't want to make mention of it?"

"Yes, he was the guy who wanted us killed, remember?"

"Is that all you can come up with? Aurora and Karpf, for God's sake!"

"I thought you asked about why she didn't say, not about how I felt. If you really want to know, I feel extremely confused."

"So am I. There also are missing elements in the case that are quite perplexing, such as why were her adoptive parents killed if they also were Frederick's biological ones? What makes sense about Clark's parents doesn't add up here."

"Which of the two pairs were murdered first?"

"Clark's—Jillian's adoptive parents."

146

"Any other siblings? Just asking."

"Thinking of it, Jillian mentioned an older stepbrother, Justin if I recall."

"Mm, what d'you think of the odds...?"

"Damn, I'm going to have to pester Klaus again. I kind of don't trust him at the moment."

"I know you're taking this all thing as some sort of conspiracy against you, but ease off, lover, we're *The Nine* remember? We own the patent on conspiracy!"

Homura was right; I was taking this all wrong. I was a hurt child releasing his incomprehension through an inner tantrum. It was time to let the storm pass and embrace the new light. We fell asleep before I finished my report. The destination was the travel.

—— o ——

# 22 – A WALK ON THE WILD SIDE

Clark had assured me the apartment was empty and that the keys were under a loose floorboard under the mat, which only made sense in terms of his meetings with Ena Karpf in the neutral zone, since he had never made it to *The Other Side*. But stranger things had happened lately.

Just to make sure, Homura knocked at the door. To our surprise, Aurora opened it and asked us in.

"I knew you would come. I crossed over in Vancouver and flew here. No-one's aware I'm on this side, not even Clark. You guys want tea?"

I had to ask.

"How did Clark know the place would be vacant?"
"I still pay the rent on it. I come here when I need my space from the craziness. It means that it's also vacant in the neutral zone—I don't go there anymore but Clark does. It takes a while to get used to the nuance."
"I guess I still pay the rent on my apartment in Seattle too, what a thought!"
"Ah ha, we can visit each other then!"
"Leave my boyfriend alone, sister!"

Homura winked at me. We agreed on a type of tea and settled in the comfortable living room. We didn't feel like talking business; being around each other was all we cared for, the quiet, the serenity, the gentle release that only happened in places with connections to the Earth, the grounding of superfluous staticity. We ceremoniously held hands for a moment of silence before lifting the warm tea to our lips. I felt complete.

— o —

"It's obvious I've got some explaining to do, but so does Ambrus; he's behind a lot of wheeling and dealing and it's time for him to fess up. That being said, you must be wondering how I ended up being selected for *The Nine*."

Me: "At this point, I suspect Nussbaum has something to do with it; he seems to have cozied up with A.I. quite nicely."

Aurora: "Possibly, but he's a tech not a mastermind. He got me in touch with Clark Meyer after Ambrus showed me the moves on crossing the lanes."

Homura: "And Ambrus would know on how to do that? You're right, he hasn't fully told his side of the story yet."

Me: "You met Ambrus in person, am I right?"

Aurora: "Yes, I had something he was hugely interested in: I was Fredrick's foster sister. He contacted me a day after my adoptive parents were murdered. I met him at his office."

Me: "You see, when Jillian was snatched from your brother's grip at *Ground Space*, he made sure to remain incognito, same with me when I transitioned from Bradford's team to his. Jillian never met him, and the first time I did was after I showed up at Homura's place on my way from Clark's house in Greenwater."

149

Homura: "I guess he had different plans for you, sister; please tell."

"He went straight to the point by explaining the gruesome details on how and why Frederick killed Clark's parents. That was when I heard about Jillian for the first time. Ambrus arranged for us to meet the next day, just the two of us. He said we had a lot in common; he was right—we went on sharing all the pertinent details of our lives. Until that point, I wasn't aware Frederick and I were step siblings. It made a lot of sense, especially after my talk with Jillian, the nuances, the small jealousies, the putdowns. I have no doubt Frederick knew, but he obviously preferred to keep it to himself."

Homura: "So, you left him that day, right?"

"No, even though Ambrus had pretty much convinced me that I had spent my life with a psychopath, he asked me to stay in touch with him. By then, we were no longer living together."

Me: "Wasn't he aware he was sending you back to the wolf?"

"First Frederick was my brother; second, he didn't kill his parents. Ambrus didn't consider me being in danger—not then."

Me: "So, what was his main reason for meeting if not to warn you?"

"Ultimately, he wanted me to work for him in keeping an eye on Frederick; it was part of incremental conditioning—he was training me to become a spy."

Me: "And how does Clark fits in all of this—time-wise?"

"He was my trainer in the neutral zone at the same time you and Jillian were put on *Travel Bureau* assignments."

Homura to me: "Isn't that the same outfit you mentioned to me yesterday—the reason why you were so upset?"

"Yes, that would be the one!"

Aurora: "Anyway, the plan was for me to stay close to Frederick so that he would trust me."

Homura: "Didn't he know about you and me?"

"If he had, we both would have been in trouble a long time ago. No, he only started to doubt my loyalty when the first mention of an impostor inside *The Nine* was made, right after your arrival, Frank."

Me: "But he couldn't have known about Homura then, so why the shooting on the waterfront?"

"It was just meant to warn you, Homura; I know for a fact that the shots weren't aimed at you—just made to look that way. No, Frank, Frederick wanted you gone, but he also lusted for your DNA. It was arranged that an ambulance would take you to one of *Ground Space Labs'* secret hideaways reserved for experimental work. Actually, he had hoped to accomplish that at the resort if it hadn't been for the two pesky feds."

Homura: "So, he must have known then that by arranging the meeting in the neutral zone, I had intended to connect with Frank."

"Yes, he learned it from me via Ambrus; we had to make it obvious to get the ball rolling. But as much as he wanted to get closer to you, Frank, he wasn't into you and Homura getting together, for the obvious reason that he sensed you were back to claim your place in *The Nine*—although, he never guessed you had *the ambers*."

Me: "So, in a nutshell, I was some sort of bait?"

Aurora: "You accepted the assignment from Klaus; you put yourself in there, so shush!"

Homura: "Glad to not be the only one to remind Frank that he creates the mess he finds himself in."

Aurora: "Blame it on his long exposure to this side; you begin loosing your compass after a while—your sense of wholeness—then you memory fades until you enter a pattern of reactionary impulses based on an insane sense of survival on the part of the crippling blindness."

Me: "Thanks for the vote of confidence, sister, I love you too!"

Homura: "You see; you can't help it, Frank!"

— o —

I was OK taking a jab or two for the right cause. I loved those two. I had found my lost sister in Aurora and my lover in her sister, a lovely tongue twister that brought warmth to my heart. Sure, it confused the hormones, but I knew where to draw the line.

Aurora: "What are you thinking, Frank, do you want to take a break?"

"No please, let's keep going if it's alright with you; I had to make a quick mind adjustment."

"At any rate, my place in *The Nine* was assured by a combination of Jillian's death and some tweaking of the A.I. algorithm. I was meant to make Frederick believe that I had taken care of it via the channels of National Security, which he trusted I had infiltrated. In reality, it was Klaus who arranged for it with a simple item of logic. He's kinda good at that!"

Me: "So, you were a double agent?"

"Correct, I worked for both Ambrus and my brother. The gay act on Frederick's part and the hopelessly lonely heart at my end played well in that context, although it was awkward at times."

Homura: "But it was clear who you worked for primarily?"

"I can't speak for Ambrus or my brother, but it was clear to me who was the fool—a hard assignment considering I was at risk of being exposed by then. I couldn't quite afford to drop the mask when Frederick was uncovered, so I had to warn him for my own protection—Ambrus was reluctant, but he understood."

Homura: "So, you weren't just being an air head—you could have fooled us all!"

"All things must reach a closure, so I decided to call the game when *Adapted Control* came to Frederick's rescue and went after you, Frank. Compound that with them showing interest in gunning Eiko down, and it was clear they had to be neutralized. I couldn't afford to compromise *the ambers* with an ambivalent position. My role as a spy was over. Because of my knowledge of *A.C.*, from that point on I concentrated on working ahead of their plans—why, for example, I was able to anticipate their presence at the café and help you out."

Homura: "When did you find out we were sisters?"

"I learned from Klaus that only twins could own the extra coding that opened the way to *The Other Lane*, so it was clear I had a brother or a sister somewhere. It took a while to find you. I figured that if Ambrus had a file on Jillian, there had to be one on me. As it turned out, it was Clark who spilled the beans on his sister by his lack of discretion in his search—I learned that from Frederick. He awoke dormant A.I. memories, sending ripples the way of *Acute Path*. Soon Markus Jones, my brother, and

Thomas Bradford were made aware of Frank and Jillian's special abilities. That was when the idea of branching out into lane travel for gains was born. Frederick was voted in as CEO of *Ground Space Labs America* soon after dissolving *Acute Watch*, and immediately started on the experiments. I'm sure you're familiar with the failures and the shutting down of the program; the rest is history. As to how I found out about you, well, Clark led me to it by showing me the paths of his previous search, except I raised a lot less dust than he did. I drilled Klaus without telling him what I was after; eventually it brought me to you, sis. No-one ever came close to knowing that you and I were twins, not Clark, Klaus, or Ambrus. But somehow Frederick learned of my visits here after his split from *The Nine*, and that's why he wanted me dead in the end."

Me: "But how?"

"Beats me; maybe he always knew, but wanted to use me to get to you and Jillian first. One thing I'm sure of, Homura, is that you never were compromised."

Me: "I'm ready for recess. One last thing though: who masterminded this whole thing, was it Ambrus since you claimed Klaus was just a tech?"

"Well, it's interesting you'd think there was a mastermind when in fact elements fell into place on their own. We simply were masters of circumstances, all of us moving along the plot as it unraveled—a lot like your assignment started with *the ambers*—a reversed case as you oddly called it. When dealing with the lanes, it's hard to know where things begin and where they end."

We smiled at each other, only wishing Jillian was with us to share the perfect moment.

# END

# OTHER WORKS BY THE AUTHOR

- The Disappearance of Olaf Swyndle   © 2016

- The Hektor Dilemma   © 2016

- Ma-l's Grand Gathering   © 2017

- Convergence of the Realms   © 2017

- Escape from Inconsequence   © 2018

- Reyes & Leeds   © 2018

- Story of a Tale-Maker   © 2019

- A Life Given, a Life Taken   © 2020

Dolosse & Writs, Eureka, California